Horrendo's
Curse

ANNA FIENBERG

Pictures by Kim Gamble

ALLEN&UNWIN

First published in 2002

Allen & Unwin
83 Alexander Street
Crows Nest NSW 2065
Australia
Phone: (61 2) 8425 0100
Fax: (61 2) 9906 2218
Email: info@allenandunwin.com
Web: www.allenandunwin.com

Fienberg, Anna.
Horrendo's curse.
For children aged 7–11 years.
ISBN 1 86508 603 7.
1. Pirates—Juvenile fiction. I. Gamble, Kim. II. Title.
A823.3

Cover and text design by Sandra Nobes
Set in 12 point Bembo by Tou-Can Design
Printed in Australia by McPherson's Printing Group

2 4 6 8 10 9 7 5 3

for stefano with love

chapter one

Once there was a boy called Horrendo who, in all his first eleven years, never said a rude word to anybody. Not even to Putrid, his pet lizard, who had bad breath and a nasty habit of spitting.

If someone stole his lunch, Horrendo would say, 'Oh dear, how hungry you must be! Why don't you take my chocolate cake as well?' Or if a person happened to race by and kick him in the shins, he would call after them, 'So sorry, aren't I always in the way? Hope you didn't hurt your foot on my shin!'

Horrendo's father tried to ignore it. His mother grew desperate.

'How's he going to get on in this cruel world,' his mother worried, 'if he can't say, "Watch where you're going, you furball swimming in slime"?'

'Or,' his father added, "you cockroach cavorting in compost"?'

Horrendo's mother looked at her husband admiringly. 'Oh, *why* didn't our son inherit your razor-sharp tongue?'

'Or my boulder-like muscles?' smiled Horrendo's father.

Now, Horrendo's dad mustn't have looked at his son closely for quite a while because Horrendo was, in fact, very strong. By the time he was ten he had muscles in his arms like rocks, and when he flexed them, they popped up and rippled in a most impressive way. (Although Horrendo never did this in front of anyone because he thought it might look threatening, and not very friendly.)

Horrendo's broad shoulders and great strength were due to the fact that he swam. Every day, he rose at dawn and went down to the sea that lay at the foot of their village. Back and forth along the beach Horrendo swam, while everyone else lay snoring. Even when a mighty storm raged, Horrendo skipped down to the shore. He loved the soft feel of the water on his skin, and the silence when he dived under the waves. Down there, beneath the surface, no one told him what a lolly-legged loser he was, or asked why didn't he eat his own earwax?

Nobody in the village noticed that Horrendo had muscles like small hills. He kept them under his jumper, and he only used them to carry old ladies' baskets filled with shopping, or to lift rocks to make pretty garden walls for the neighbours.

'Oh, why did that old witch have to choose *my* son?' Horrendo's mother wept each day. 'What did *I* do to deserve such a punishment?'

Horrendo would fidget uneasily and cast his eyes around. 'She's not an old witch, mother, she's a Wise Woman.' He chided her gently, in an anxious way, reminding her that Gretel the Wise Woman had ears everywhere (so to speak) and loathed any kind of rudeness. 'It's always best to say nothing, mother dear, if you can't say anything nice. Especially in the case of a Wise Woman.'

Horrendo's mother snorted disdainfully. 'Wise, my fish-faced aunt! *Wise?* To put a Charming spell on my only son? In this treacherous world? Pah! Run off and lock up Putrid for the night, before I call you worms for brains and feed you to the birds in the forest.'

Now, truth to tell, Horrendo didn't always enjoy being polite. Sometimes he too hated the Wise Woman who had singled him out with her Charming spell and made him so different. Sometimes he wanted to say, 'Why don't you go boil your head, you mean-spirited, pudding-faced meddler!' especially when Bombastic, that bully in his class, pulled his hair. But the words never reached his lips. Instead of a curse there was a compliment, all pretty and neat in his mouth like a rosebud.

It was just luck, that's what it was. *Bad* luck. Because on the day Horrendo was born, the Wise Woman came to town.

Now I must tell you that just beyond Horrendo's village there grew a forest where owls hunted and snakes slithered. If you took the narrow path from the village and followed it deep into the woods, you would come to a clearing. And there, surrounded by

a carefully tended herb and vegetable garden, was the cottage of Gretel the Wise Woman.

Gretel rarely visited the village, as the food for her table and the herbs for her potions all came from her own garden. For company she had a Siamese cat which lay like a dropped rug around her shoulders, even in summer. But whenever Gretel *did* put on her walking shoes and visit the village, something mysterious always happened.

On the day of Horrendo's birth, Gretel was buying thread at a stall at the market. A boy rode past on his bicycle and, spying the cat lying lazily on her neck, he shouted, 'Fat cat, go chase a rat, *splat*!'

The Wise Woman gave him a look that pinned him there on the road. 'Enough of this village and its rudeness,' she said quietly. She pointed a finger at the boy and then at all the houses surrounding the square. 'A child will be born today, and although he'll have the power of speech, he'll be unable to curse or swear. Although he'll have the power of movement, he'll be unable to hurt or maim. And then, you will see.' And Gretel turned back to considering colours for her threads.

Horrendo was indeed born that Tuesday, and he gurgled happily as he lay in his mother's arms. She hoped and prayed for two years that the spell wouldn't work, but when her son finally spoke his first words, she knew the worst, and her heart sank.

'Thank you so much, Mummy, for that delicious

mashed-up turnip. It was really very nice but you shouldn't go to all that trouble just for me.'

There had never been anyone in the village like Horrendo. The books in the town library boasted only scallywags and rogues. Everyone had sharp faces and tongues like whips, and no one said 'thank you' or 'please', for the villagers lived in a dark world ruled by pernicious pirates and the terrors of the sea.

chapter Two

Every child in the village was afraid of the pirates. No matter how tough and rude the children were taught to be, no matter how many classes in Sword Fighting or Insult Invention they'd attended, they all trembled at the thought of the skull and crossbones. So did their parents, and their aunts and uncles and grandfathers. Because every autumn, the pirates sailed in with their black flag flying and swooped down upon the village.

You could see them coming from miles away. The tall ship rose up on the horizon and slid forward,

silent, like the dark coming down. There was nothing you could do to stop it. You might as well try to stop your own shadow. Then you'd hear them. The cursing and fighting on board ship was enough to wake a giant squid on the ocean floor.

The pirates didn't try to catch the village by surprise. There was no need. They trained their massive cannons on the town and then strolled in with their cutlasses and gold teeth flashing and took all the boys turned twelve. 'Snatch the small fry!' they'd roar. 'Grab the grizzler! Lasso those lads!' And the boys would be hauled up by huge hairy hands, one by one, easy as pulling up grass.

Turning twelve in that village was like going through an earthquake or swimming against a tidal wave. Because only if you managed to survive two years on board were you allowed to return home. And few boys ever did.

The ones that *did* come back told dreadful tales. Children put their hands over their ears so as not to hear, and old people closed their eyes. Grown men in the town wanted to forget their nightmare at sea. Horrendo's own father went about pretending it had never happened—except sometimes you could hear him shouting in his dreams, 'Get yer whip off me, you filthy felon, or I'll wrap it so tight round yer neck yer eyes'll pop out like boiled eggs!'

Horrendo remembered the year Mongrel and Scamp returned, skinny as skeletons and scarred all over with whiplash. When they tried to talk, people ran away, but Horrendo didn't want to be rude, and stayed. His eyes grew round and his mouth fell open.

'You should've seen it, men falling down like flies all over the deck,' Mongrel whispered. 'If they didn't get up again in thirty seconds, the Captain threatened to throw 'em to the sharks. "One less mouth to feed," he'd say, and give that evil smile of his, real deadly.'

'That's right,' said Scamp. 'Men keelin' over from sword fights and starvation and overwork. Shiver me timbers, how they'd laugh when us new boys came— we'd do all their cookin' and swabbin' of the decks and climbin' to the crow's nest. They only want us young ones, see, 'cause we're easier to train and can't put up as much fight.'

It had been like this as far back as anyone could remember. Horrendo's village, with its sheltered bay, had always been the pirates' favourite for raiding and plundering, and some years there were so few males left in the village that men from other islands were invited to row over, please, and set up house there.

No one remembered a time when the Captain of the pirates *hadn't* ruled the sea. And didn't he have his spies all over the islands? Devil man, people muttered about him among themselves, a demon you couldn't kill.

The books in the village were full of the Captain's ghoulish deeds, but Horrendo and his class hadn't dared to open one since Bombastic read out loud to them from a chapter called 'Cannibalism: A Human Diet at Sea'.

Horrendo, like all the other boys, began school at four years of age. Girls started later, at six, and attended school on the other side of the village. Horrendo often watched wistfully as groups of girls strolled across the square. Sometimes, they'd look wistfully back. But friendships between the sexes were not encouraged in the village, as close attachments of *that* kind, the elders said, only caused heartache later on.

In their first year, to toughen their nerves and prepare them for life at sea, the boys were taught Deadly Insults and Rude Remarks. Then, to assist them in the fight against capture (a hopeless task, most teachers agreed, but what else could they do?) the boys had lessons in Herculean Headlocks, Oar Throwing, Playing Dead, and Jumping on Pirates from a Great Height.

In their senior years boys could specialise in Petrifying Pets, where they trained their pet to leap at the attacking pirate and bite, poison, tickle or paralyse him. Horrendo's parents had bought Putrid for this reason, but the lizard seemed interested only in spitting at its owner.

Horrendo's favourite subject at school was Hiding.

He tried hard at all the other subjects and, because of his strong muscles, he got quite good at Oar Throwing. But if he was told to throw the oar *at* someone, he fell apart. Anyway, as far as he could see, Hiding was the only subject that had any results.

Take the time those two boys, Vile and Hellhound, escaped capture—it was the year Horrendo started school. The boys had hidden under an overturned rowing boat, right next to the ship! None of the pirates had thought a village boy would have the courage or wit to come so close. Vile and Hellhound became legends in their own time, and their cunning and success gave everyone hope.

Still and all, there was no getting round it: the thought of turning twelve was a depressing one. It was like putting brackets around your life, or worse, a full stop. Even Horrendo, who thought it only polite to make the best of things, felt down about it sometimes.

'You just have to learn to enjoy each day,' Horrendo's father often remarked, 'until the last one dawns. And boy, will *that* be a dog dropping of a day. The scummiest page you'll ever turn. The dirtiest chapter in life's adventures. But don't think about all that now. *I* don't. Relax. Enjoy!'

One morning, some months before his twelfth birthday, Horrendo went down as usual to the sea. He swam up and down the beach, out beyond the waves, but he didn't feel the springy rush of freedom in his heart that he used to. In fact, his arms felt like lead, and he thought he might as well sink like a stone to the bottom. He'd be late for class if he didn't get a move on, but just then he didn't care.

The twelfth year in a boy's life was the worst, everyone said so. Because very likely it was his last.

As Horrendo lay floating in the sea like a wet paper bag, an idea came to him. It was such a good idea that his arms suddenly felt energetic again, and a flourish of hope made his heart pump wildly.

Why didn't he hide *under* the water when the pirates came? It would be brilliant! Maybe he'd hide under their very own ship! He'd practise holding his breath every morning when he came to swim—why, he'd get so good at it, he'd probably turn into a fish!

He did a couple of practice runs and then raced out onto the shore, hardly stopping to dry himself properly. He couldn't wait to tell everyone. He couldn't wait to start training sessions.

When Horrendo arrived at the schoolhouse, his hair was still wet.

'Listen, everyone,' he panted, interrupting his teacher who was giving a lesson on Petrifying Pets, 'I've got a great idea for saving our lives.'

'Sit down, Horrendo,' said his teacher. 'I'm surprised at you, bursting in here like a bee-stung bull.'

'Bird-brain!' yelled Bombastic.

'Dog-breath!' sang out Mischief.

'Be quiet, you smelly bunch of ingrown toenails,' said the teacher. 'I'm not interested in what you have to say, Horrendo. Take your seat and stop dripping all over the floor. Now, as I was telling you, the black widow spider is a venomous character with a nasty habit of eating its mate. The female has red markings and her bite is quick-acting, paralysing its victim in no time. I hope you all brought your Petrifying Pet along this morning? Hmm? Any black widows, death adders?'

Horrendo had to sit through sea snakes, stinging jellyfish, pythons, and a tarantula in a tall glass jar.

'The tarantula's hairs have tiny spines that can make the skin itch and burn,' a skinny boy called Hoodlum told them earnestly. The huge spider was cradled in his palm as if it were his favourite biscuit. 'When threatened, a tarantula scrapes hairs off its abdomen and showers them on its enemy. Of course, right now my tarantula is very relaxed.'

'Looks about as dangerous as a dead fly,' called out Mischief.

'As lethal as Granny's knickers!'

'Terrifying as toe jam!'

Hoodlum's face grew red with rage and his fingers curled into a fist. He shook it manfully at the class, and shouted, 'Shut up, you—' then suddenly howled with pain. Unfurling his fist he revealed his crumpled tarantula which had apparently felt threatened.

Before lunch the children were told to work individually with their pets, while the teacher walked around and looked at them.

Horrendo kept an anxious eye on Bombastic who sat opposite him. Bombastic was doing experiments with his poison dart frog, Pest, trying to elevate its levels of venom. He put hemlock leaves on the desk for it to eat, but that just made the frog sick. So he gave it little jabs with the sharp point of his pencil. This seemed to work, causing the frog to swell with fury. Bombastic laughed with delight and threw it at Horrendo, just to make sure.

Luckily Horrendo was quite flexible from all his swimming activity and ducked nicely, the frog sailing just inches over his head and landing with a small damp thud against the wall.

'Quick, *get* it!' yelled Bombastic, tearing after the

furious frog. He ran through the desks, stepping on people's shoes and pets with such reckless haste that snakes and bird-killing spiders and earwigs scrambled free. Such a mess and tumble there was that Horrendo had to wait until lunchtime before he could tell his classmates of his wonderful idea.

'So all we have to do is hold our breath,' Horrendo said as they sat down to eat their dreadful sandwiches. 'You know, we'll have to train of course, starting off with ten seconds, then twenty and so on. We'll spread out along the rocks, hiding under the water, coming up just for a moment, then pushing ourselves under again. No one's done it before, they'll never guess! Besides,' added Horrendo, 'I reckon those pirates would have terrible eyesight from all that squinting at the sun, don't you?'

'I think you've got earwigs in your brain,' Bombastic snorted. 'Hold your breath—what kind of wimpy excuse for a fight is that?'

'Yeah, lolly legs!'

'Jelly custard!'

'Go eat your own earwax, snotrag!'

Horrendo wandered away. He walked for quite a while, not really thinking about where he was going. When he got tired he sat down on the sand and looked at the waves rolling in.

Wasn't it always the same? Why did he imagine even for a moment life could be any different? That anyone would listen to *him*, old lolly legs. The sandwich in his mouth tasted like mouldy fish eggs.

That's because it *was* mouldy fish eggs. Most mothers in the village carefully kept some food to rot and gather fungus, to prepare their eleven-year-old boys for the kind of food they'd be eating at sea. For a mad moment, Horrendo felt tempted to spit out the revolting mess and damn the lot of them. But then he thought of his mother and her lovingly labelled bags of lunch fillings—earthworm relish, slug seasoning, cockroach paste—and he felt his throat obediently open and swallow.

'Well, *I'm* going to hide underwater,' he told himself valiantly as he stood up. 'There's no harm in saving my*self*, is there?' He looked around quickly after making such a bold statement. Then he went for a speedy swim and a holding-breath training session before returning to school.

chapter Three

'Hey, *psst*! Horrendo—over here!'

It was a fine early summer's day and Horrendo was sitting by himself on the school bench, as usual, eating his lunch. He looked up and saw a group of boys huddled around Bombastic, hurling cockroaches at each other. Over to the right were Mischief and his gang, absorbed in burying their lunches. Straight ahead stood the huge old oak tree, which had never said a word, as far as Horrendo knew.

He went back to eating his sandwiches.

'Quick, snail brain, come here!'

Horrendo saw a face pop out from behind the tree and quickly disappear again. Rascal's face. Well, fancy that! And what a kind invitation!

Horrendo strolled towards him, looking vaguely up at the sky, so no one would notice him. Rascal grabbed his shirt and pulled him down so they were both crouching behind the wide trunk of the tree.

'Can I help you with anything, Rascal?' Horrendo began politely. 'Have you lost your lunch, I still have half—'

'Listen, I been thinking about your idea,' Rascal said, peering all around him as he spoke. 'You know, the hiding under the water trick. It sounds like the best idea anyone's gunna have.'

Horrendo could feel something warm starting in his chest, then spreading all through his body. It was like hot milk and honey before bed, or something melting fragrantly in the sun. He smiled at Rascal.

'Not that I want any of the others to know,' Rascal said quickly. 'I mean, they'd just throw rocks at us or something. They'd call me a lily-livered fool. But, see, I been thinking about your idea all these last weeks.'

'Oh Rascal, why didn't you say anything? I'd have been so pleased to—'

'Yeah, yeah, I know,' snapped Rascal. 'But I gotta think about things a while first, see? And now it's summer and all, and our time's coming nearer—well, I'd like to join up and start your training sessions.'

Horrendo beamed. The warm feeling was now like electricity in his veins and he wanted to grab Rascal's hand and run down to the sea and save him, all in the next three minutes.

But he took a deep breath and said, 'Okay that would be wonderful, we've lost quite a bit of time but I'm so pleased to have your support and you won't regret it I'm sure, so if *you're* sure then it will be very rewarding to—'

'Just tell me when to meet you, brain drain,' hissed Rascal.

'The beach at dawn,' Horrendo whispered back.
They both stood up.

'And don't act like you know me at school,' Rascal
flung over his shoulder as he walked hastily away.

'No, no,' Horrendo called back. 'I wouldn't dream
of it.' But as he walked into the classroom, he said
quietly to himself, 'No, I'd never tell anyone we were
friends. Never.'

The word painted itself across his mind over and
over. And every time he looked at it, the warm milk-
and-honey feeling came back.

Most mornings when the sun rose and lit up the sea
like a treasure chest, Horrendo and Rascal went

swimming. Horrendo thought he'd better start at the beginning and teach Rascal a few basic strokes.

'We'll be in the water for a couple of hours,' Horrendo told him, 'and if the pirates see us they're sure to give chase. You'll want to know how to get around in the water, fast, to duck and dive and hold your breath.'

Rascal had a lot to learn. He could barely do anything but float when they started, but after just two weeks, he was fair at freestyle and quite brilliant at breast stroke.

Horrendo was delighted with his progress. 'You are a splendid student,' he said, clapping Rascal (gently) on the back.

'Shut up, shark breath,' replied Rascal, but he grinned shyly back.

Rascal worked on his diving, too. This wasn't strictly necessary for escape-from-capture strategy, but Horrendo said nothing about wasting time because he could see that Rascal was enjoying it. And there must have been something special about his diving style, something that belonged to the sea and its creatures, for he brought the dolphins.

Every day they came in a group of four, swooping through the water, leaping and playing like children. Rascal swam with them and, after a few days, he tried grabbing hold of a dolphin's fin, and glided through the water at great speed. Soon Horrendo and Rascal were swimming like dolphins themselves, as they raced and frolicked in the sea.

But the holding-your-breath-under-water sessions went a little more slowly. Rascal had a bad chest and often suffered from bronchitis. When everyone else got a cold and threw it off, Rascal had to go to bed for a week. Once he'd nearly died.

'We've got to cure that chest of yours before the pirates come,' his mother was always telling him. 'You'll be shark meat within the week otherwise—all those draughts and the freezing ocean.' She gave him garlic sandwiches every day, because the Wise Woman had told her it would help ward off a cold. Garlic also kept away vampires, Rascal's sister told him, which was definitely a plus. (Rascal's sister, Blusta, was studying Medicinal Herbs and Plants, and often visited the Wise Woman at her house, so she'd know, wouldn't she?) In any case, Rascal's bad chest made him a bit breathless, especially if he was coming down with anything.

For their training sessions, the boys swam out beyond the waves, keeping to the line of rocks that spread out under the towering cliffs. This was treacherous as the reef was covered with sharp little barnacles and rocks like daggers. But they needed to have something to cling to when they popped up for air and rest, and there were small inlets around corners where they could hide most successfully.

Rascal's breathing had improved with the swimming, but still he found it hard to fill his lungs completely without coughing.

Horrendo was a very patient teacher and spent a lot of time thinking of jokes and topics of conversation each night to keep Rascal's spirits up during the day. Rascal had to sneak out of the house before dawn because his mother wouldn't approve of all that swimming in the cold sea.

'You'll catch your death,' she'd say, and very likely lock him in his room if she knew of his early morning escapades.

But Blusta knew about the secret swimming training, and would meet Rascal on his way out of the house. 'Take your garlic and ginger,' she'd whisper, 'and walk three times widdershins around your towel before you get dry.'

Rascal had never felt better in his life. His breathing was deeper and slower—and yet it wasn't just that. For the first time he dared to hope he might live longer than twelve. All his life before now, he'd silently agreed with his mother. He'd look down at his hollow chest and skinny ribs and imagine shivering to death with one of his fevers on board a pirate ship. His uncle had gone that way and he'd always imagined he'd do the same.

By the end of summer, Rascal could hold his breath for thirty seconds. At the end of the season, he was staying underwater for sixty.

'That's excellent, golly gosh, what stamina, tremendous courage, cracking skill!' Horrendo would cry. He was very encouraging.

'Not as good as you, frog face,' said Rascal.

Horrendo's record was two minutes, it was true, but he didn't like to brag. 'Don't worry, we can dive deep and swim far in sixty seconds,' Horrendo assured him. 'We can make that first little inlet to the south in under fifty, then we'll lie low. We'll be fine—we'll be like Vile and Hellhound, legends in our own time!'

And who knows, they just might have been and everything may have turned out very differently ... but when you're dealing with pirates, plans seldom go as expected.

On Horrendo's twelfth birthday, his mother lay in bed with her face to the wall. It wasn't until lunchtime that she sat up and called to her husband, 'Oh, tell me, what'll we do when the pirates come?'

'Hush, don't talk of that now,' said her husband. 'Let us enjoy these last months with our son. There'll be time enough to think of those stinking sea-dogs.'

'But in the autumn you know they'll come and snatch him quicker than you can say, "Hoist the mainsail, you snivelling swine."' And she moaned dreadfully, wringing her hands.

Horrendo noticed that the skin round her nails was quite worn away, what with all the worrying and the wringing. 'Mother,' he said, 'you must put Hurtle's Hand Cream on your poor palms. I use it every night after I've cooked dinner and washed up and mopped the kitchen floor.'

Just then Horrendo's father made a strange noise. His cheeks were swollen scarlet and little popping sounds were coming from his mouth.

'You see? You see?' said Mother. 'Our son won't last five minutes with those pirates, so polite and considerate as he is. What will you bet he'll be there worrying that their arms might ache when they give him fifty lashes with the cat-o'-nine-tails? Bake their bones!'

There was a loud crash as Horrendo's father ran out and leapt onto the kitchen table. He began jumping up and down, up and down, shaking his fists in fury and shouting, 'Pickle their eyes in vinegar!'

That was the thing about Father, Horrendo thought as he and his mother followed him into the kitchen. Just when you imagined he wasn't paying attention to anything, or noticing if you said 'good morning' or 'there's a dead body in the garden', he'd explode like a firecracker.

'You'll see,' Mother went on, her eyes like yoyos as she watched her husband's demented leaping. 'They'll pick our son up just as if he was an old sheet and they'll throw him over their shoulders.'

'Fry their toes in turpentine!' boomed Father.

'Then they'll hurl him onto their ship and make him work like a dog.'

'Grill their gizzards in oil!'

'They'll whip him and beat him until he can't get up any more, whereupon they'll slice him into pieces with the nearest cutlass, easy as pie. That's what will happen to our son. That's what.'

The table broke.

Father dropped down and stared at the ruins of his life.

Horrendo looked at his parents. They were standing together, their shoulders bowed. Their faces looked pale and hopeless, like a cloudy night without the possibility of stars.

Horrendo frowned. 'You two shouldn't worry so much,' he said softly. 'It's bad for your health.'

But even as he turned away, he felt the shooting bolts of panic start in his belly (making him hurry to the toilet) that always came at the mention of the pirates.

Horrendo was the last in his class to turn twelve. He'd gone to all the other boys' birthday parties, which were more like funerals, truth to tell. No one enjoyed these events, but it was tradition for all the boys to attend. Eight in all they had celebrated, and very depressing affairs they'd been, too.

Horrendo had wanted to invite Blusta to his party because he'd been fond of her ever since she'd winked at him from across the square six years ago. But his father said it wouldn't be right, not until he came back. (*If* he came back, thought Horrendo.)

At the party, the boys sat around Horrendo's kitchen table discussing the capture of last year's twelve-year-olds.

'Every one of 'em gone,' said Mischief gloomily.

'You see what happened to Wart's poison dart frog?' Hoodlum moaned. 'Took one look at those pirates and ran off like a scared rabbit. Useless git.'

'Mine'll be different, but,' said Bombastic, crossing his fingers behind his back for luck.

A nervous, knuckle-cracking boy called Rip sighed. 'And what about that pathetic Jumping from a Great Height? If Sneak and Tiger couldn't flatten a pirate, what hope do *we* have? Best in the school they were and they missed their target, landing on Tiger's cranky old dog.' He sighed again. 'All gone.'

'All gone,' they droned together as if reciting a prayer.

'Would anyone like another slice of meatloaf?' Horrendo asked, breaking the dismal silence. 'I baked it with mushrooms picked fresh this morning,' he added hopefully.

But no one did.

When the boys got up to leave, Rascal grinned at Horrendo. 'All gone except us, eh?' he whispered at the door.

Horrendo smiled back, but he felt uneasy. It wasn't nice to keep a secret from people. It was like a lie, wasn't it? He wished Rascal wouldn't insist on silence. It made him prickle all the way down his back, as if he had ants running along his spine.

As if the Wise Woman was right there, behind him.

chapter four

The first day of autumn was a Sunday. Horrendo's mother crossed it off the calendar with a moan, and shook her head. 'Now the waiting begins. We never know if they'll come *early* autumn or late. It might be tomorrow or it might be three months.'

'That's right,' said Horrendo's father briskly. 'That's why every day we still have our son is one extra for us. Look at it that way, treasure of my heart!'

But Horrendo's mother was not to be silenced. 'I *hate* this waiting. It's like the sun never coming out properly—always the hint of storm in the air. Blast those brigands who blemish our life!'

Horrendo watched his mother's hand-wringing, and frowned. He wished he could tell her about his plan, and how she wasn't about to lose her only son. But he knew she didn't share his faith in Hiding, and how could he risk her stopping him? He wished he could make her smile, too, but he couldn't think of one single joke that day. He was worried, and not just about the pirates.

Early in the morning, Horrendo had raced down to the beach as usual, expecting to see Rascal doing his laps. But the sea had lain empty and calm, like an iced cake nobody wanted to cut.

Horrendo had peered into the water—any second now and wouldn't he spot Rascal's dark head popping up?

Horrendo had even grinned for a moment, thinking what an excellent job of hiding his friend was doing. Beating his own record, wasn't he?

But after another minute, Horrendo had grown worried. He'd dived in and swum underwater with his eyes open. Searching all around the rocks, he'd explored every inlet they'd studied, swimming far out beyond the waves. Horrendo had finally given up and dragged himself out onto the shore. He'd looked around on the sand for Rascal's clothes and towel, and found nothing.

As Horrendo had trudged back home, he'd decided that Rascal probably couldn't escape that morning. Maybe his mother had woken early. Or maybe he'd set off that home-made burglar alarm of pots and pans Rascal's mother arranged every night before going to bed. (Rascal hated that alarm.)

But the next morning Rascal again failed to show. And when Horrendo got to school, Rascal was absent. Later, as he was walking home in the afternoon, Horrendo saw Blusta hurrying across the square. He raced after her and asked if she wouldn't mind stopping one moment and telling him where Rascal was please?

'At home in bed with his mucus,' replied Blusta. 'He's come down with one of his infernal colds. Nose streaming like a running tap, a whistle in his lungs louder than a kettle boiling. I've put marjoram in his bath and a warm brick at his feet. Oh, Horrendo, you wouldn't believe our luck would you—autumn, for goodness' sake, and those perishing pirates here any day now.'

'So he'll be staying in bed tomorrow, too?' asked Horrendo, dashed to his bones.

'He will indeed, and all the week as well. He needs constant nursing with that chest of his, and Mother and I will be keeping an eye on him every minute, don't you worry!'

Blusta turned to go but then spun round on her heel. 'I wish you good luck with the swimming, Horrendo. Rascal might not make it, but I hope with all my vital spirit that *you* do.' And her smile was like the sun bursting through.

'Why *thank* you, Blusta, that's so very nice of you to say and extremely poetic too, and I hope you don't catch Rascal's cold but stay healthy and strong in your, ah, vital spirit during the winter.'

'I will, too,' Blusta nodded, 'what with all the garlic I've been nailing on our door and cloves hanging round our necks!' Suddenly she frowned and shook her fist in the air. 'Those beastly pirates—why, if they lay a hand on you, I'll throw pepper in their eyes and shove scorpions up their noses. I'll twist their wicked greasy guts for them and pull out all their teeth, I'll—'

Just then Horrendo's mother appeared at his elbow, laden with packages. 'Oh, Horrendo dear, do walk home with me and carry these heavy bundles. I won't have him to help me for long, you know, dear,' she added to Blusta, smiling sadly, while she thrust the apples and potatoes and turnips into her son's arms. As Horrendo dragged along the square with his mother, he glanced back wistfully, wondering what other terrible and torturous pirate-whacking plans he would have heard from dear Blusta if his mother hadn't come along right then and interrupted.

At home, Horrendo fed Putrid (who spat at him), did his homework (lassoing the garden furniture) and tried not to irritate his mother. But his eyes stung and his throat felt tight, as if someone had taken his lasso from the leg of the chair, thrown it around his neck and pulled.

Each morning after that Horrendo still looked for Rascal at the beach, because he couldn't help hoping. He'd stand at the top of the sand dune and peer out towards the horizon. No Rascal, no pirates. Well, thought Horrendo by Friday, so far so good: if we can see the week out without an invasion of pirates, Rascal just might make it.

But on Sunday morning when Horrendo climbed the sand dune, he saw a strange figure standing by the shore. Slowly he crept down the hill, and as he grew closer, dread filled his heart so that he nearly ran back.

Although he had not made a sound, the figure turned and called to him. The cat draped around her shoulders showed its claws.

'Horrendo, come and speak with me, I have something for you.'

The cat hissed as Horrendo stepped forward. His legs felt heavy, as if he were walking in quicksand. But his mouth, as usual, opened and closed politely.

'Good morning, Wise Gretel,' he said cheerfully. 'What a beautiful day, and how particularly well your dear cat is looking. My! what fine strong claws he has, and may I say what a pleasant surprise it is to see you both on this brisk, sunny morning.'

How perfectly awful that cat is, thought Horrendo all the while he spoke, just look at its nasty pinched face and sly eyes. Why do I have to stand here in this freezing wind, babbling to this woman who's ruined my life?

As Horrendo rambled on politely, unable to stop, Gretel rummaged in the large pockets of her dress.

'Horrendo,' she said finally, placing a small silver box in his hand, 'I want you to take this gift to sea.'

'But I'm not *going* to sea,' he burst out. 'That is to say, dear Wise Gretel, I didn't mean to contradict you and I know it's not polite to keep secrets but you see I plan to hide and *escape* the dreaded pirates if you don't mind but thank you so much for this . . . er . . . it is very kind of you to think of me—'

My jaws ache with smiling, he thought, but I want to spit like Putrid.

'Keep my gift safe, now,' said the Wise Woman, 'it may help you survive the pirate ship.'

'But I'm not *going* on the pirate ship—' Horrendo looked at her face and stopped. 'Oh, excuse me, I'm so overwrought at the moment what with the pirates about to arrive and Rascal's cold and . . . please, dear lady, what is this beautiful gift if that's not too impertinent of me to ask and if you'd rather not say why of course—'

'Inside the box is a fine powder of crushed herbs. I've put a strong flavour-enhancing charm on it, so just one grain will be enough to bring out the magic in any meal.'

Gretel suddenly put a finger under his chin and lifted his face until his eyes were looking straight into hers. He felt dizzy for a moment, as if he were falling. In a low voice Gretel said, 'The charm is very powerful, Horrendo. Use it wisely. You will know when it is time.'

Horrendo was so transfixed by the Wise Woman's eyes that he hardly heard her words. Rather, they vibrated inside him like a drum. He felt like a fish hooked and lowered into her power, and there in her sea-blue eyes he saw himself as if he were looking into a mirror—his babyhood, his mother, his dreaded last birthday. But then he glimpsed something that made him catch his breath and swim up suddenly, back into the fresh cold breeze.

'Yes,' said Gretel quietly, 'they have come. Look!'

He turned and saw the ship that had been reflected in the Wise Woman's eyes. There, on the horizon, its black flag flying and its bow cutting through the blue like a knife, was the ship he'd been dreading all his life.

'Pirates!' whispered Horrendo, but Gretel had vanished, leaving only her strange gift still clutched in his hand.

Horrendo took one more glance at the ship, hardly able to believe it was real after all these years of imagining, then stuffed the gift deep into his trouser pocket and dived straight into the water.

chapter five

Horrendo swam underwater, round the cliff that hugged the beach, to the southern inlet tucked in behind. The sea dropped sharply from the reef, and Horrendo could dive down and be covered in a fraction of a second. From here he could see everything, and he shivered as he watched the ship move ever closer.

Horrendo's trousers and shirt were heavy in the water but there was no time to remove them. He ground his teeth. That Wise Woman, she'd almost spoiled everything. This was exactly *not* how he'd planned it.

He kept just his nose and eyes above the water.
Like a crocodile, he waited there, his gaze fixed on the
bow of the ship. Now he could see clearly the massive
figurehead of the cobra rising at the front, and the flag
with the skull and crossbones flapping in the breeze.
He saw men jostling on deck and a figure high up,
swinging on the rigging like a spider.

Horrendo's heart was pounding. He fingered the box
in his pocket. The contents would probably be sopping
—what happened to herbs when they got wet? Probably
useless, by now. Anyway, why should a mess of flowers
help him, when the Wise Woman herself never had?

A wave of sound washed over him. Big male voices,
singing, swearing, their voices tearing up the air like
thunder. He could see a huge tower of a man standing
on the fo'c'sle, peering through a telescope. Horrendo
ducked underwater, his heart beating fast. As he
counted the seconds, his mind flicked over what he
had seen—long black beard, chest like an oak tree.
How would any of the boys have a chance against that?

When Horrendo popped his head back above water,
the ship had drifted in, so close now that Horrendo
could see the men's beards and a glint of gold as an
earring flashed in the early morning sun.

'See to the anchor, Squid!' shouted the pirate with
the telescope.

He must be the Captain—surely the man was the
biggest on board.

A jolly-boat was lowered, then two small dinghies.
Horrendo watched as ten, maybe twenty men climbed

down the ropes and headed over the waves, surfing their way in to shore.

'It'll be a good meal we'll 'ave tonight!' boomed the big pirate. The men pulled the oars through the water at a great pace. 'Fresh grub for dinner, and many young hands make light work, eh mateys?'

The men laughed and then the big pirate turned and looked back at the ship. He gave a kind of salute and a nod.

A lone man was left standing at the fo'c'sle, watching. He didn't wave back, just stood still, legs astride, as if he were a piece of wood carved straight from the ship.

Horrendo felt goosebumps crawl up his arms. It wasn't that he was cold—although the water *was* icy—but there was something about that silent man at the bow, something unreasoning and cruel that made him shiver. He hoped *he* wasn't the Captain.

Two hours Horrendo waited in the freezing bay. He spent a good deal of it swimming about amongst the rocks to keep warm. He had a nasty feeling that the wooden man on board had piercing eyes and never once stopped searching the surface of the sea.

While Horrendo swam he thought about the boys in his class—how right now they'd be throwing oars and hurling their petrifying pets, and how their hearts must be hammering inside their chests at the sight of those big burly men.

Whenever he came up for air he could hear faint screams and roars coming from the village, and his stomach turned over. He pictured the pirates raiding everyone's iceboxes, stealing chickens and vegies from their gardens. His mother would be trying to save her new shiny saucepan, and Blusta—oh, please don't let them hurt Blusta! He felt such a rush of sad fondness for them all—even Bombastic with his pathetic dart frog—and he ached to know if Rascal had still been in bed when the pirates came swooping in.

And then, when he came up for air for the thousandth time, he saw the first pirate striding back over the sand. A boy bumped along over his shoulder, kicking furiously. Then another pirate came, and another, and soon they were so close Horrendo could see the faces and bodies of the boys they carried. There was Rip, grinding his knuckles into the pirate's neck; then came Mischief, Hoodlum, Rowdy and Wildman. They'd given in, their heads lolling upon the pirates' chests. Demon bobbed along next and last, at a distance from the others, came Bombastic. He'd been swung over his captor's shoulder like all the others, but was still pounding the man's chest with one fist.

'Flies are bad today, eh!' grinned the pirate and gave Bombastic such a clout on his legs that he cried out with pain.

That was all of them, thought Horrendo, his nose barely above the water. All except Rascal. He closed his eyes for a moment and dived down deep. Please, please, he prayed, please don't let me see Rascal. Please let Rascal go. Make it that Rascal hid so well no one could find him, make it . . .

Horrendo surfaced, gasping, and saw the pirates shoving the boys into the rowboats. Parents, aunties, sisters were running down to the shore, yelling insults and shaking their fists.

But then, making way through the parting crowd, was the big bearded pirate Horrendo had first seen. And over his shoulder flopped Rascal, lifeless as a sack of potatoes.

The pirate dropped Rascal into the boat and began rowing out past the waves. Behind the broad back of the man, Rascal sat up straight as a fence post. He gazed intently at the sea, his hand raised to shade his eyes. Peering in the direction of the cliffs, he suddenly stared right at Horrendo.

Fear raced like lightning through Horrendo's heart. He'd been seen! Before he ducked under the waves he noticed Rascal glance away, a small smile on his lips.

What a friend! thought Horrendo wildly. How loyal, how noble—going to his death without flinching. Horrendo could feel his throat stinging and salty tears streamed down his face, splashing into the sea.

A fierce loneliness came over Horrendo then, like a cloud moving over the sun. He was free, he was saved, but instead of joy he felt only a longing to be with his friend, and for things to be different.

Suddenly he shot up into the air like a dolphin and did a backward flip. 'Ahoy there, you forgot about me!' he cried. 'Over here, O enormous bearded pirate, if you don't mind that is and I'm so sorry about you having to backtrack and so on, creating all this bother, only—'

He swam a little way to meet up with the boat, and as he was hauled up by a big meaty hand, Horrendo clapped Rascal (gently) on the back.

'Is this the village idiot?' the pirate asked Rascal wonderingly.

Horrendo grinned.

'You might say that,' said Rascal, and grinned back.

chapter six

'Ey, you annoyin' little cockroach, bring me my breakfast *pronto* or I'll squash yer with my fist like the bug that you are!' shouted the First Mate.

Horrendo scurried up from the galley wishing he did have six legs, or maybe a hundred arms would be more useful. Maybe it would be better to be a centipede than a cockroach, actually . . .

'What the blazes are you doin' standin' there in a daze?' bellowed another pirate. 'Where's my devilled eggs?'

'Where's my French toast?'

'Where's my rum?'

The crew lounged about on deck—it was a warm sunny morning and they lay against piles of rope and old boxes, picking their teeth and scratching their toes.

'Not a bad little lot, these ones,' said the pirate Squid, who'd found an old piece of meat the size of a golf ball between the gaps in his back teeth. He flicked it at Bombastic who was hurrying by with cups of rum for the sprawling pirates. 'Do what we tell 'em, no answerin' back—'

'Aye, they'd want to behave after the whippin' we gave that one,' said Wicked, scratching the tattoo on his arm. He jerked his head in Mischief's direction. 'No more cheek we'll get there, eh?' And the pirates' laughter was like stormwater rushing down a drain.

Horrendo looked at Mischief as he bent over a pirate, handing him his tea. His thin back was striped with huge scabs where the wounds from the lash were healing. Horrendo noticed him wince as he straightened up, holding another cup of steaming tea for the next pirate. As he limped away, Squid suddenly shot out his leg and Mischief tripped, spilling the boiling liquid down his own arms and chest.

'Hahaha *haaa!*' the pirates burst out laughing, slapping their huge thighs and digging each other in the ribs.

'What a clumsy coot!' they chortled.

'Bloomin' silly bungler! He'd poke 'is own eye out scratching 'is head!'

'Good one, Squidman!'

Horrendo looked on as Mischief bit his lip, trying not to cry out. Horrendo knew better than to go to his aid—Mischief would only get another kick.

He glanced at the other boys, pulling ropes, folding sails, scrubbing the deck. They too looked briefly at Mischief, but didn't dare say a word.

Yes, thought Horrendo heavily, this certainly was the scummiest page he'd ever turned; the dirtiest chapter in life's adventures.

On the first day, when he'd been assigned to kitchen duty, Horrendo had opened the silver box of herbs. Amazingly, even after his two desperate hours in the sea, he'd found the fine green powder was still as dry as dust. He had sprinkled a little in his palm, and the smell that had wafted towards him was so delicious that the saliva started in his mouth and his eyes watered. 'Just one grain is enough,' the Wise Woman had said, 'to bring out the magic in any meal.' Why Gretel thought it so important that the pirates enjoy their food Horrendo couldn't understand, but he fervently hoped it was true, as it seemed to him that only a miracle could save the boys on board.

Since then he had faithfully added one grain to each feast he prepared for the pirates, praying that this was 'the right time'. For surely things couldn't get any worse?

By the time the boys had been on board for three weeks, it seemed like forever. From sun-up to sundown the boys worked like slaves. They carried, fetched, lifted and hauled. Rascal had to climb up to the crow's nest each day and cling there, staring out at the empty sea. He was terrified of heights (that's why the Captain had chosen him), and when there was a gale his fingers iced up and went numb, making it hard to hold on.

'I'm slipping!' Rascal called out at night in his dreams.

Horrendo had made twenty new fishing lines out of bits of old rope, and from the leftovers he knitted a pair of gloves for Rascal. He told him to rub his hands with grease first, to keep in the heat, and then slip them on. But when the Captain found the gloves he told Rascal they'd make him 'soft' and threw them into the sea.

At night the boys all slept together down in the one small cabin. But they were lucky if they could get to sleep at all. They lay on rough canvas mats, with not a blanket or sheet in sight, listening to the drunken brawling and singing of their captors. Sometimes they heard each other sob, but no one ever mentioned it in the daylight.

No one mentioned Pest, either, Bombastic's poison dart frog, which he'd managed to smuggle aboard. It was rumoured that the Captain had a peculiar and particular hatred of amphibians. ('Stupid idiots can't decide if they're fishes or lizards!' he'd once remarked.)

The Captain loathed any kind of indecision, calling it 'namby-pambying', and he was known to run his pirates through with a sword, easy as blinking, if any of them hesitated in battle. So Bombastic kept Pest hidden away in his leather pouch, deep inside his waistcoat.

Pest had shown neither courage nor loyalty when his master had been captured, preferring to burrow deep into the boy's pocket and lie still, pretending to be a marble. Bombastic told Pest 'he'd better lift his game or he'd feed him to the Captain', but he'd whisper to it softly, calling the creature 'Pet' instead of Pest, when everyone else was asleep.

What with raiding the village and Horrendo's new fishing lines, there was an abundance of fresh food on board. And never had the pirates eaten so well. Not a weevil in sight, not a plate of old catfish or kelp to be seen. They could hardly believe the aromas and flavours that Horrendo conjured up each day.

When Horrendo handed a plate of prawns to the First Mate on that fine sunny morning, he grabbed the plate with both hands and threw them down his throat, hardly bothering to chew. Horrendo stared, amazed, as the small mountain of prawns disappeared in a flash.

The man eats exactly like a dog, thought Horrendo. He remembered how Tiger's hound gulped and swallowed in just the same way, never stopping to chew. They're just not human, these men, he puzzled, and yet they must have been once . . .

'Oi, get over 'ere,' yelled Squid. 'Never stand idle on this ship, young shark feed, or you'll be found floating face down out there!' And he pointed at the wide blue sea.

How clean and peaceful it looked, thought Horrendo, and a stab of longing pierced him as he remembered his early morning swims.

'I said, come 'ere!' Squid shouted and actually got up.

Horrendo hurried over, bringing French toast.

'So sorry to be slow, sir, and making you wait when I'm sure you're hungry after all your hard work.'

'Don't give me cheek, boy, or—' and he drew his finger across his throat.

'Oh no, sir, I'd never do that, and I hope you enjoy your toast to which I took the liberty of adding a glorious syrup I just happened to cook up, using a dab of butter and honey and a little rum, sweetened with brown sugar if you please—'

Squid rolled his eyes and shouted, 'Shut up, you irritatin' little sea slug!'

He poked Horrendo hard in the ribs with the barrel of his long pistol, leaving him breathless and making him almost drop the toast.

'Oh dear, aren't I clumsy running into your poor pistol that way?' gasped Horrendo. 'My, my! I nearly lost your breakfast too, so sorry—'

'The devil take that boy,' snarled the First Mate. 'Makes you want to swat 'im, doesn't he? "Please" this and "thank you" that—what cloud does he live on, the varmint? He'll drive us all mad.'

'Yeah,' said the pirate called Dogfish, picking his nose. 'Specially the Captain.'

'Mmm,' answered the First Mate, glancing around uneasily. He watched Squid take a huge bite of French toast. The pirate closed his eyes and chewed, looking as if he'd just died and been sent to heaven.

'Cor,' he mumbled. 'Bloomin' marvellous!'

The First Mate's mouth was watering. 'Cooks like a dream, though, doesn't he?' he whispered to Squid. 'Have you ever had food like this before?'

Squid squinched up his face, trying to think. (He didn't do this often, so it took quite a long while.) 'Never all these years at sea. But once, now don't go tellin' anyone I said this, once I remember me mamma makin' somethin' sweet like this.'

'Aye,' said the First Mate softly, a faraway look on his face. Then he reached out and grabbed Squid's second piece of toast, quicker than you can say 'bottle of rum'.

'Oi, you great tub of lard, that was *my* toast!' yelled Squid. 'Give it 'ere, or I'll stick this sword so far down yer throat it'll clip yer toenails for yer!'

And Horrendo watched the two pirates leap at each other, fists flying. Now I'll have to bake another batch, he thought gloomily. But as he trudged back down to the galley, he decided it was worth all the work to see those scowling pirate faces soften for a moment when their mouths were full.

The Captain, however, was another matter. That man wasn't very interested in food, preferring to live on rum and ship's biscuits 'like he'd always done'.

'Just try to hold your tongue,' Rascal had whispered to Horrendo one day. 'Say nothing, is that so hard? Don't you *see* the way he looks at you? He'd chuck you over the side with his empty bottles before you could say "grog-faced villain". Why, that one'd watch the sharks gobble you up, and laugh.'

Horrendo shivered. He remembered seeing the Captain for the first time—standing alone on the fo'c'sle the day they'd been captured. He'd been right to fear him. The Captain was a tall man with long hard muscles like ropes. There was not an ounce of anything comfortable or fleshy or soft on him. He was like the sword in his belt, sharp and one-sided, unacquainted with compromise.

But when Horrendo cooked up a feast, it was not in his nature to leave anyone out. 'Isn't it rude to ignore a person?' he'd ask himself. 'Wouldn't they feel disliked and rejected? The thing is, though,' he'd go on, 'I don't really *like* the Captain, so which is more important, honesty or kindness?' This was the type of question that Horrendo wrestled with for hours and that sometimes made him burn the toast. He wished there was someone he could ask, but, although he tried, no one ever quite seemed to get the point.

Horrendo baked thirty more loaves of bread that morning (word got around that the French toast was out of this world), marinated twenty kilos of prawns in garlic and ginger, and fried seventy-six soles in butter and flour. Horrendo found that the galley was actually quite well set up, much better than his own kitchen at home. The pirates stole not only boys, money and food but all the latest kitchen equipment as well. So Horrendo threw out the old containers of worms and jellied eels and seaweed that he found in the icebox and began to stock the pantry with goodies.

Later that morning he went to check the fishing lines and nets hung over the side and haul in the catch. The First Mate agreed to help him because a young white pointer was caught in a net, impossible for Horrendo to lift.

'Sorry to ask you when you're busy, sir, but what would you say to a nice shark's fin soup? Mr Squid was telling me about it, sir, said he'd tasted it once in his travels to the Far East and I've been wanting to try it if you don't mind, sir—'

'Get outta the way, prawn head!' panted the First Mate as he pulled in the net. But Horrendo could see the way his eyes lit up at the mention of the soup.

When Horrendo presented the Captain with his meal (politeness won after all), warning him to, 'Be careful, sir, it's very hot, not that I should be giving *you* orders, ho ho, just a little joke, sorry please that is, er, thank you, sir', the Captain threw the steaming plate into Horrendo's face.

'Stop your wretched gabbling, you IDIOT!' he roared.

Tears of pain filled Horrendo's eyes. They spilled over, mixing wetly with the soup thickening on his cheeks. He tried to wipe the mess away but the

Captain grabbed his hands. He turned them over like two small sardines.

'Soft,' he sneered. 'Useless as a baby's. Never done a decent day's work in your life, eh? Look at you, standing there snivelling like a silly newborn. Hey, lads, have you ever seen such a blithering baby?'

Horrendo lowered his eyes to the floor, but before he did he caught a glimpse, right up close, of the Captain's face. Hard as marble it was, or petrified wood—no feeling could carve a trace there. A deep vein throbbed in the middle of the man's forehead. Horrendo couldn't stop his hands from trembling and jumping in the Captain's cold grip.

'Listen here, boy,' he hissed, pulling Horrendo so near that he could see the flat black eyes under their lids. 'If you say "sorry" or "please" to me one more

time, I'll string you up to the mast and let the gulls peck out your eyes. That's a promise.'

And he pushed Horrendo away, sending him flying over a bucket of slops with a single jab of his fist.

That night, after Horrendo had served dinner and washed up and done his hour's watch, he dropped onto his corner of the mat and fell fast asleep. How eagerly he looked forward to that nightly swim into dreamland. It was such a relief to be unconscious.

He was dreaming of the dolphins that often followed the boat—he loved watching them leap and dive for the leftover fish he threw them—when a sound woke him. He turned over to see Rascal sobbing into the mat.

Horrendo clapped him (gently) on the back.

'Go back to sleep, peabrain,' snuffled Rascal.

Horrendo left his arm there. 'Please don't worry, Rascal, I promise I won't irritate the Captain any more, cross my heart and hope to die, well, that is, not really *die*, but that's just how the expression goes, doesn't it? Anyway, our future will be bright because one day, when we get home, I'm going to marry your sister, if she'll have me of course, and you can come and live with us, that is if you'd like to, and we'll make a different life. Maybe we'll move far away—'

'What about my mother?'

'She can come too, certainly, why naturally! And very welcome she'd be but if you don't mind could you ask her not to bring her burglar alarm and her

cockroach mincer? And of course my mum and dad
would come too—'

'How would we make a living? Or find a house?
Where's the money coming from? Travel is
expensive—'

Horrendo frowned. 'I'm working on that one but
don't you worry, the thing is to think about the future
not the present. When you're out there on the crow's
nest, look up not down, and think of all the
possibilities the big blue sky can hold—'

'Hurricanes and lightning, that's what.'

There was silence for a moment as they both
thought of Rascal climbing the ropes, and Horrendo
remembered how tiny he always looked up there, like
a little black ant, as he crawled into the crow's nest.
They lay for a moment, listening to the 'whoo, whoo'
of the wind outside, and Horrendo tried not to think
of the terrible vein that threatened to explode at the
centre of the Captain's forehead.

But then Rascal blew his nose on the mat and said
softly, 'Listen, dog breath, even if I don't make it, I
hope you do get to marry my sister. I really do.'

And somehow, even with the moan of the wind
and the swearing of the pirates out on deck, they both
fell asleep again till dawn.

chapter seven

The next day was a sulky grey, but calm. The boys
went about their duties, swabbing decks, sharpening
swords, hauling sails. Each day was the same, except
for a whipping or a fight, and the boys grew thinner
and more silent with every week that passed.

Horrendo scurried around the galley, cooking up
better and grander banquets for the pirates. The boys
were given only the leftovers (of which there weren't
many, as the pirates, especially the First Mate, often
licked their plates clean).

After dinner, when the Captain had retired to his
cabin, the men liked to sit around under the stars and
sing. The boys almost enjoyed this time of the day, as
they could flop down and stretch out their aching
muscles. But you could never drop your guard for
long, as Bombastic bitterly complained, because the
Captain's behaviour was as unpredictable as a lightning
strike. Take the time Pest nearly became shark bait.

Bombastic had let his frog out on deck to get a
little fresh night air when the Captain suddenly
stomped back up. It was past midnight and no one had

ever seen the Captain out so late. Pest froze, but he couldn't help glowing there like a bright red ruby. Frantically, Bombastic glanced around for somewhere to hide him. Spotting Squid's glass of rum and water, he quickly plopped Pest in and spread his hand over the top, keeping him there until the Captain was safely back below decks.

Poor Pest had never been the same since. The frog had a trembly hop and a bleary eye, and was always trying to get at someone's rum. He'd developed a taste for the stuff, Bombastic swore it, and no mistake.

Meanwhile, there was no doubt that the pirates had developed a taste for Horrendo's cooking. But one night when he came out on deck with a jam tart for everyone's dessert, Horrendo found Dogfish lying flat on his back, moaning.

'Ah, give it a rest,' Squid yelled at Dogfish, and kicked him casually in the kidneys. 'Why don't yer shut yer gob and give us all a bit of peace!'

'Yeah,' agreed the pirate Buzzard, who was strumming on a guitar, 'you sound like a cow with a bellyache!'

'That's because I've got one—ooh, me guts, they're twistin' inside—'

'Pew! Oi, stinky, shove off and go hang over the side!'

'Yeah, stop blowin' off an' move yer smelly carcass!'

Horrendo put down the tart and crept over to Dogfish.

'Where does it hurt, if you wouldn't mind telling me, sir?' he whispered.

Dogfish looked at him. His face was white and sweat bubbled on his top lip. 'Here,' he said meekly, and pointed to his stomach just above his navel.

'And here, sir?' asked Horrendo politely, pointing to the middle of his chest.

'Yeah, sharp pains shoot up, makin' me burp an' all.'

Horrendo nodded. 'Indigestion and flatulence, I'd say, Mr Dogfish, if you don't mind my being so bold. Do you get it often, sir?'

Dogfish nodded, dying for a chance to complain. 'Ever since I was a kid.' He lowered his voice even further. 'Well, ever since I came on board, that is. Used to burn me up somethin' terrible and they'd make me go up the crow's nest with me guts just about killin' me.'

Horrendo put his hand on the man's stomach and patted him. 'That must have been very hard for you, Mr Dogfish, sir, what with you feeling so torn up inside.'

Dogfish looked at Horrendo. 'Are you havin' me on?'

'No,' said Horrendo earnestly, 'I think it's amazing you survived this hard life with that poor ailing stomach of yours, sir. You must have wanted to lie down many times and just give up the fight.'

Dogfish bit his lip and sighed, and words tumbled out in a rush from having been dammed up for so long. Horrendo sat and listened and nodded, sighing with him.

'But if you lasted the first two years, Mr Dogfish, sir, if you don't mind my asking, why didn't you go back home then?'

Dogfish gave a loud snort. 'I dunno, after two years I sort of forgot what it was like not to be at sea. And then it wasn't the greatest life on land either, I can tell yer. Same sort of fightin' for yer daily bread and we never 'ad any money and me dad used to whip me just the same. At least 'ere I've got some mates, even if they are a bunch of dunderheads.'

'Oi, what's that brat doing up at this time of night?' yelled the First Mate. 'If the Captain sees 'im there'll be hell to pay. Get below, ya silly mooncalf!'

Horrendo whispered a hurried goodnight to Dogfish and promised to brew him up a remedy that his mother made back home. Then he ducked down to the cabin and out of sight.

He didn't want the Captain seeing him. He didn't want to look at that hard wooden face if he could help it. Those blank eyes, like the eyes of a shark, scared Horrendo more than anything he'd seen on board— more than the whip or the First Mate in a temper. No, he never wanted to have those eyes on him. Not ever.

It was a week later that Rascal leant out over the wobbly rail of the crow's nest and shouted, 'Ship on the horizon!'

No one even looked up. The men were too busy devouring lunch: lobster mornay with crab soup to start.

'The soup's out of this world!' cried Squid.

'Wait till you've tasted the lobster!' yelled Buzzard.

'My guts are in heaven!' added Dogfish poetically. 'That home remedy's done me a power of good!'

The First Mate passed wind loudly and began to pick his teeth. 'Aye, best part of the day, this,' he murmured. 'Big meal, big sleep,' and he closed his eyes with a contented sigh.

The boys grinned tiredly at each other. If that meant a rest for them too, then they agreed.

'Ship on the horizon,' Rascal called again. 'And it's flying a skull and crossbones!'

Still no one stirred.

Suddenly there was a loud bang as the Captain swung back his cabin door and stepped out onto the deck.

'You lazy bunch of lubberlegs, didn't you hear the boy?' he bellowed. 'Look at the lot of you! Never have I seen such a fat lot of swine slurping over their swill—nothing but slobs. What's that you're guzzling?'

The pirates all stared at each other, their faces pale as the clouds overhead.

'Well? Well?' roared the Captain. 'Have you lost your voices as well as your piratical backbones?' No one spoke. Every pirate and boy froze in their place. 'Too busy thinking about your stomachs, eh?' said the Captain. 'Well, I want to know who's responsible.'

The Captain unsheathed his sword and stalked around the ship. He stopped every now and then, pointing the tip of his sword at someone, letting it dig

into the flesh of a belly or a chest for a moment, then
moving on. The silence was awesome, with everyone
holding their breath and only the sound of the waves
slapping against the sides.

Bombastic, who had been leaning against a wooden
crate, shifted his weight suddenly and sent the pot
holding the remains of lobster mornay crashing to the
floor. He jumped in fright and fell back on Dogfish,
ending up in his lap.

The Captain pounced on the boy like a panther.
'Will you look at the little boy on his daddy's lap! How

sweet—ah, ya pathetic lot of whimpering *mongrels!*'
The Captain spat and looked down at the mess of
white sauce that lay congealing on the deck. He
pointed his sword at Bombastic, letting it rest lightly
against his throat. Bombastic gulped as Pest burrowed
down even deeper inside his pocket.

'You've gone soft, the lot of you,' the Captain
said, looking around. His voice was an animal's snarl,
and his yellow teeth were bared. The sharp tip of the
sword pressed deeper into Bombastic's throat. 'Look
at the mess you've made,' he said to the boy. 'Maybe
I should make an example of you. Cut off your
clumsy legs so you can't trip and *hurt* yourself.' His
sword moved slowly down to Bombastic's trembling
knees and slid across the skin, leaving a red welling
wound. 'If you hadn't given the men that muck,
you wouldn't have made this mess.'

'It's all *his* fault,' cried Bombastic, thrusting a finger
at Horrendo. He jerked back from the sword and
picked up the pot. 'See? Lobster. Soup and tarts and
French toast. He feeds this to them all day!'

The First Mate scowled. The pirates looked down
at their toes.

'Come here, you,' the Captain hissed at Horrendo.

But just then Rascal, who'd been climbing
frantically down the ropes, cried out, 'It's a pirate
ship! They've got their cannons out. They're closing
in on us!'

The Captain swung round to face his First Mate.
'Hand me your telescope, before I tear the guts from

your belly. Dogfish, Squid, Goose and Buzzard, man the guns! Crew, swords at the ready.'

'It's the Blue Devils!' cried the First Mate from the bow.

A moan went around the ship like a wind rising.

'It'll be watery graves for us,' whispered Dogfish.

'Ooh, I don't want to die!' groaned Goose.

'Shut up, you pack of milksops,' shouted the Captain. 'If I see anyone hiding, they'll get *my* sword through their necks. First Mate, give the boys fire buckets and tell 'em to watch out for flames. NOW!'

Horrendo, Mischief and Hoodlum crouched together at starboard. The Blue Devils sailed swiftly over the waves, heading towards them as surely as an arrow flies to its target. The deck shuddered under their feet as a cannonball whizzed past a boy's ears and hit the second mast. A flash went up and the mizzen burst into flame.

The boys flew about with buckets, their hearts thumping. The pirate ship was so close they could make out the huge wooden figurehead of the devil rising up from the bow. Then the air darkened suddenly as the ship slid up alongside and the shadow of the Blue Devils fell over them. Grappling hooks flew through the air and their ship was held fast. The boys trembled. Rip cracked his knuckles. They plastered themselves against the sides, eyes squinched closed, while the Devils leapt over them and onto the ship.

'Take that, ya cutthroat hound!'

'Gerroff, ya grog-faced villain!'

Swords clashed so steadily that the sound of ringing metal vibrated in the air like cymbals. Horrendo put his hands over his ears, but somehow it all looked even more frightening without the noise. He saw Dogfish forced back against the mast and Buzzard dodging two swords at once; Squid had both arms full of pirate and a leg holding another one down. (That's how he got his name, thought Horrendo, tentacles everywhere!)

The battle raged all over the deck, savage and bloody. To Horrendo and the boys it seemed that the

Blue Devils would soon be masters of their ship. Men were down all over the deck, and Goose's pinkie finger and Buzzard's earlobe had been sliced clean away. Wicked swiped the air wildly with his sword, the skull tattoo on his arm bobbing about as if it were alive. The Captain was nowhere to be seen. The boys threw buckets of water at the flames but small fires broke out faster than they could run.

Bombastic kept climbing up on the rigging and leaping down onto the backs of the Devils, but once he missed and his bottom landed on a burning crate. He stopped leaping after that and crouched against the sides with the rest of the exhausted boys.

Suddenly the Captain appeared from nowhere. He had the Blue Devil captain in a headlock, and held a pistol to his head.

'Put down your cutlasses, you Devils,' he bellowed, 'or I'll blow his brains out.'

The Devils glared and muttered and cursed, but slowly, one by one, they dropped their swords.

'Now get off my ship, you bunch of craven chicken hearts!' He watched their retreating backs and added to the First Mate, 'Take the prisoner down below and heave to.'

Just then the captain of the Blue Devils kicked his captor in the shin and wrenched free. He made a desperate leap for his ship still lying alongside. But the grappling lines were being taken off and the ships were drifting apart. With one leg perched on the edge of his own ship and the other dangling behind, the Blue

Devil hovered for just a second before he toppled,
falling like a stone into the widening corridor of deep
dark sea.

Men from both crews rushed to look over the sides.
But there was nothing to show where the Blue Devil
met his end, not even a bubble rising to the surface.

'I *told*'im he should've 'ad swimmin' lessons,' said
one of his crew. 'But could ya ever tell 'im anythin'?'

'Not that one,' sighed another. '"If I was meant to swim, I'd 'ave fins on me back and a tail on me bum", that's what 'e always told us.'

As the Blue Devils sailed away, pulled by a gusty wind, the Captain rounded on his men. 'As for *you* lot,' he sneered, '*you* are the craven chicken hearts. What kind of fighting was that? You didn't deserve to win. We could have lost our ship. White-livered milksops, stinking cowards! You fight like a bunch of mewling puppies. What's got into you?' His eyes narrowed as he looked around at the crew.

Shark eyes, thought Horrendo. *Please don't bite!*

His glance stopped and lingered for a moment on Horrendo. Then he turned on his heel, making his way back down to the cabin. 'Bring me a bottle of rum,' he called over his shoulder, 'pronto!'

'Aye aye, Cap'n,' called the First Mate, tripping over Buzzard who was lying, knocked out, over a coil of rope.

chapter Eight

Hours later, when the sun had set and the ship was drifting on a slow breeze, the pirates lay stiff and sore on the deck.

'Where's my poor pinkie?' wailed Goose for the tenth time. He was on all fours, searching the splintery ground.

'Where's my earlobe?' moaned Buzzard. 'If anyone sees it, could you let me know? I just want to bury it the right way. Say goodbye an' all.'

Squid fiddled with his own ear. 'What's the use of this itty-bitty piece hanging on the end, anyway?' he asked, pulling on the lobe. 'I've always wondered that.'

'Me too,' said Dogfish. 'I wonder about a lot of things. Like why are there deadly stonefish in the sea and stingrays and box jellyfish that kill you in four minutes flat? I mean to say, what purpose do they serve?'

Several pirates nodded, looking out at the dangerous ocean.

'And why are there so many different types of spiders?' another voice whispered in the dusk. 'Haven't you ever wondered that? I mean, just one or two kinds would be enough. You could have, say, yer tarantula and yer huntsman—'

'Where's my poor pinkie?' cried Goose.

'That's eleven times,' said Squid.

'My loyal pinkie, been with me all my life,' Goose went on. 'It picked my nose when only a little finger would do—you know those hard crusty bits you get up the back? And it was me old pinkie that wore Mamma's ring. Gave it to me when I was just a kid, she did.'

Dogfish rubbed his stomach and winced. 'And what's the point of a man's existence, do you ever think about that?'

'Aye,' said Buzzard. 'I ponder it of a mornin' when I'm hangin' over the side.'

'Aye,' went on Dogfish. 'Shiver me timbers, me belly aches like fire.'

'Yeah, an' I'm bleedin' to death over 'ere,' said Buzzard, who also had a nasty gash on his leg. 'Soon I won't have to worry about anythin' at all—earlobes or spiders or what's the point of nothin'. The dark'll come down like a curtain and nobody'll even notice.'

'Aye,' agreed the pirates, and sank into a heavy silence.

The First Mate shifted his bulk and fell heavily onto Squid's shoulder.

'Aaaargh, watch it, you great oaf!' squealed Squid. 'I got a broken collarbone stickin' up there like a dagger. You'll snap it off!'

'Ah, go swallow yer head,' muttered the First Mate.

Just then a mouth-watering aroma filled the air. The pirates stared in disbelief as Horrendo trotted towards them, a tureen of soup sending up curls of delicious swordfish- and noodle-flavoured steam.

'I don't believe it!' cried the First Mate, tears in his eyes.

'I've just died and gone to heaven!' crowed Dogfish.

'*This* is the point of a man's existence,' sobbed Buzzard.

'Well, isn't that the truth, Mr Buzzard, sir?' said Horrendo, ladling out generous portions of soup. 'And look at your poor ear, oh, sir, that must hurt so dreadfully, and your leg is quite cut up. It's a wonder you're conscious at all. I'll just go and find some bandages—'

'And look at my poor hand,' Goose called out plaintively to Horrendo. 'See? Lost me pinkie. Where's my poor pinkie?'

'That's twelve,' said Squid.

'Oh, Mr Goose, sir, what a terrible injury, does it ache awfully?'

'Somethin' dreadful,' moaned Goose, nodding hard. 'And now it's gone all cold and sort of icy round the edges.'

Soon the pirates were all moaning and some were weeping and Horrendo ran down to the cabin and woke the other boys to help him. They scurried up and down with bandages and hot water, and Horrendo doled out soothing words and gentle pats on the shoulder. He swabbed the pirates' wounds with rum and tore up old shirts for bandages and listened and comforted them as they talked.

By the time the moon rose, sending a shiver of silver over the lilting sea, the men were quiet and sleepy.

'That soup was just what the doctor ordered,' murmured Dogfish. And he actually smiled at Horrendo.

'I remember a soup like that, far back in a distant time,' said Squid in a low voice.

'When I was . . . a kid,' Goose said hesitantly, 'my mum sometimes made me soup when I was sick. I remember how it would trickle down my throat, all warm and nourishin', and everythin' was all right.'

'Aye,' sighed Squid. 'Remember when she hugged you if you was hurt?'

Bombastic nudged Rascal in the ribs and giggled. Rascal ignored him. He was listening intently.

'Aye,' nodded the pirates.

'Remember *girls*?' whispered Dogfish.

'Oh, *aye*,' the pirates said dreamily and grinned at each other.

A crash and a tumble of swear words startled them all out of their reverie. 'Remember WHAT?' came a harsh voice out of the gloom. A figure lurched from the shadows and towered over the men, swaying slightly on his feet.

'What's that SMELL? What are these dirty PLATES doing all over the deck? What's this TALKING?' The Captain glared wildly about him, an empty bottle of rum clutched tightly in his hand.

Horrendo got quickly to his feet. 'The men are wounded, sir, and please, sir, I can see quite a deep cut just above your elbow if you will let me bandage it for you, sir—'

'Shut up, you nitwit, or I'll cut your arms off.'

The Captain stared at Horrendo, who took a pace back. The boy glanced briefly into those blank shark eyes. He remembered for a moment how he'd looked into the Wise Woman's eyes: that was where he'd seen his life unfold. Now, in this short glance, he felt he was seeing his death.

The Captain threw down the bottle and watched it smash into a thousand pieces on the deck.

'Oi, watch out for me poor leg!' Buzzard cried out, before he had time to think.

There was a terrible silence then, and in the quiet, Horrendo heard the men drawing in their breath.

The Captain took a step towards Horrendo so that his nose was only an inch away. The vein in his forehead swelled alarmingly. He reeked of rum and a stale bitter smell that came from some deep, empty place inside him.

'Poor leg, eh?' he hissed, still staring at Horrendo. 'Did you hear that, boy? Gone soft, haven't they, boy? All thinking only of their own comfort, not respecting their Captain, eh? And who's to blame for that, little boy?'

The Captain grabbed Horrendo around the throat and spat into his face. 'Look around, boy, look up at the stars, 'cause this is the last night you'll be sleeping under them.'

Horrendo choked, his throat working under the steely hand.

'I'm fed up with your cooking and all your donkey-brained talk. I don't want to hear another "please" out of your stupid mouth. Tomorrow you walk the plank —and a nice little meal you'll be for all those hungry sharks. I bet they'll say *thank you* nicely. Ha ha haaa!'

And he swayed off into the shadows, back towards his cabin.

chapter Nine

Horrendo lay on the mat in the dark. It was past two o'clock, but who cared about sleep? Not Horrendo. He lay thinking about his life, which was shortly to end. There, in the pitch black of the cabin, his eyes stung as he remembered the pirates and how they'd left their work and gathered around him after the Captain had left.

'Don't worry,' the First Mate had said, 'he'll forget all about it in the mornin'.'

'Aye,' agreed Dogfish. 'Pickled as a gherkin he was.'

But for once Horrendo couldn't say a word. The men watched him silently as he went below. The boys followed, their heads bowed as if he'd already died. They pressed his hand and shook their heads. When they were curling up for the night, they all tried to lie close but pretended that they were squashed, and jostled and punched each other for comfort.

One by one the boys began to snore. Everyone, that is, except Horrendo and his friend Rascal.

'The thing is,' Rascal whispered into the quiet, 'there's nowhere to hide on a ship.'

'That's right,' agreed Horrendo heavily. 'Nowhere.'

They were quiet again, until Horrendo said, 'You know, Rascal, I don't mind walking the plank. I mean, at least I'd be swimming again—it's what I do best, if you don't mind my saying so and I hope you don't think I'm boasting or anything like that. But we're out in the middle of nowhere, aren't we? Even if I was the best swimmer in the world, how long would I last in the open sea with no land in sight?'

Rascal nodded sympathetically, then, realising Horrendo couldn't see in the dark, said, 'You might last a day, maybe two, but then there's the sharks—'

'Sssh, please,' Horrendo whispered suddenly. 'Excuse me for interrupting, but I can hear something . . .'

Footsteps passed the boys' cabin and padded on towards the Captain's. There was a low rumble and then the voices rang out, clear as gulls squawking.

'Why, that's a treasure map, Cap'n!' It was the First Mate talking and he seemed very excited. But after that the voices dropped and the boys couldn't make out the words.

Horrendo hopped up and bounded out of the cabin.

'Come back!' hissed Rascal. 'If they see you—'

'What, they'll make me walk the plank?'

Rascal sighed and went after him, tiptoeing down the narrow passage.

The door to the Captain's cabin was closed, but if they stood close, they could make out every word.

'Been waiting twenty years to get my hands on this treasure,' the Captain's voice growled. 'Old Blue Devil's grandfather buried it—enough gold coins to keep us and our children for the rest of our days.'

'But we ain't got no children—'

'Shut up, fathead, I mean *if* we had children. And now we know where the treasure's buried, don't you realise?'

'Is that what you was doin' while we was fightin'? Lootin' around on the Blue Devil's ship? Aye,' there was a tone of admiration as well as fear in the First Mate's voice, 'you've got a nerve and no mistake.'

'That's why I'm a Captain and you're only a fathead. You do nothing, you lot, but stuff your faces. Now listen, the treasure's buried on one of these islands only fifteen miles from here. See, due east.'

'But how do you know the loot's still there? Blue Devil must've raided it himself by now.'

The boys heard the Captain give a short laugh like a whip cracking. 'He tried once five years ago and lost most of his men. They're not called the Shipwreck Isles for nothing. Nearly lost his ship. The rumour on the seas is he was too lily-livered to try it again.'

There was silence for a moment and then a crackle of paper. Rascal turned on his heel, ready to run. But what they heard next made both of them freeze.

'But Cap'n, no wonder he lost his men—look, we'd have to sail straight through the Scorpio Strait!' protested the First Mate. 'You know what the winds are like there—damn hurricanes through a tunnel. And the currents are killin'. Waves bigger'n houses. We'd never survive it!'

'Ah, stop your whingeing,' the Captain replied. 'Don't you want to be rich?'

'Of course I do, but the men aren't fit enough, sir,' the First Mate went on. 'There's scarcely one could reach the masthead right now—an' those who can move are all knottin' and splicin'. Our rigging's been cut to pieces.'

'That's easy—we'll use the boys.'

'They'll need to spend all day pumpin'—the hole in the bow is taking in water. Anyway, with those winds they'd be blown off before they were halfway up the shrouds. They'd be droppin' into the sea like bluebottles!'

They heard a thump like a fist pounding the table.

'But look, Captain,' the First Mate said in excitement, 'if we sail south and do a loop, we could come at the islands safely and avoid the straits!'

'No,' came the Captain's voice, cool as ice. 'That would mean sailing an extra hundred miles. East we go, and don't say another word about it to the men or I'll cut out your tonsils and feed 'em to the gulls.'

The boys, listening outside, could practically hear the First Mate's teeth grinding.

'You'll lose yer ship,' the First Mate growled.

'We'll ease the sheets and sail by the jib,' answered the Captain.

'You'll never get anyone up there to set sail. The men would be blown away like flies in those winds.'

'Stop complaining, you ninny. I told you, I'll send the boys, starting with the one that climbs the crow's nest—what's his name?'

'Rascal.'

'Aye, I'll get Rascal to go first and show the others how to climb the ratlines and reef the sails.'

Outside the door, their bare feet on the splintery floor, the boys shuddered right down to their bones.

'But he'll die doin' it, sir.'

'So what if he does? After him we'll get another, don't you worry. Plenty more where he came from.'

'And then you'll start on the men,' muttered the First Mate.

But it seemed the Captain could hear only the tinkle of the thousand gold coins that would soon be his. 'I'm going to get that treasure, and nothing's going to stop me,' he said sharply.

There was another silence, and then the boys heard a huge sigh.

'Well, sir, um,' the First Mate's voice was slow and hesitant. 'Perhaps it would be a good idea to let the

boy Horrendo stay on board durin' the crossing.
I mean to say, the men will grumble about the
conditions sir, and at least Horrendo's cookin' keeps
'em happy—'

'Keeps 'em soft, you mean! No, that one walks the
plank at dawn and no more talk about it or you'll go
with him.'

'Aye aye, sir.' The First Mate sighed again and the
boys heard his footsteps approaching the door. Without
waiting to blink they raced back down the corridor
and into their cabin.

Breathing hard, they threw themselves down on the
mat. They both lay shivering in silence, the awful
words replaying in their heads. Finally Horrendo
clapped Rascal (gently) on the back.

'There's only one thing for you to do, Rascal. At
least this is what I think and of course you don't have
to agree—'

'Come with you tomorrow?'

'Yes. Somehow you'll have to make a running jump
for it. You have an excellent freestyle stroke, and you've
got more chance of surviving the fifteen miles
swimming with me I would say, if you don't mind my
being so—'

'I'll do it,' said Rascal, his voice trembling. 'I'll do
anything not to stay on board this stinking ship and
climb those stinking ropes.'

'Good, that's excellent, Rascal!' whispered
Horrendo. 'I really think we'll have a sporting
chance—fifteen miles isn't too far—'

'As long as we don't get swept away by waves huge as houses—'

'We'll dive under and hold our breath—'

'Or meet one of those white pointers—'

'We'll swim faster—'

'Or get bitten by the sea snakes—'

'We'll keep our eyes peeled—'

'Or stung by the box jellyfish.'

After a moment Horrendo said softly, 'What about the other boys?'

'What about them?' asked Rascal.

'Well, we can't leave them here to be picked off like flies, one after the other, can we?'

'Can't we?'

'No.'

They listened to the snores all around them. 'Get away, you louse!' cried somebody, as he fought off a nightmare. 'Go stick your head up a drain,' muttered someone else in his sleep.

Horrendo blinked back tears of affection.

'But they'd never come with us,' burst out Rascal. 'They can't swim well, maybe they wouldn't make it.'

'They won't make it here, either. I'll help them, I'll find a way.'

'But what have they ever done for you? What about Bombastic?'

Horrendo blew his nose on the mat. 'Things have got to change, Rascal. It's all gone on too long—your father, *his* father—everyone's lives ruined.' Horrendo flexed his arm muscles in the dark. He felt strong suddenly, just as he did when he used to swim every morning. An idea was floating at the corner of his mind, lighting up his vital spirit (as Blusta would say), making his heart thump wildly.

'We've got to get *organised*, Rascal,' he said, sitting up. 'We've got to stick together. If it's only you and me, then sure, *we* may survive, but what will change really? We'll just be two boys like Vile and Hellhound, legends in our own time.'

'I wouldn't mind being a legend, but,' said Rascal quietly.

'Yes, but the pirates will still come back every year, and the parents will mourn, and we'll all go on hating and fearing each other. If we stick together and *all* escape, why things will change forever—we'll show them they can't fool with us any more!' Horrendo took a deep breath, and put his hand on his friend's shoulder. 'Otherwise, Rascal, what will we be surviving *for*, that's what I want to know. What will there be to come back *to*?'

'A soft bed,' whispered Rascal, shifting uncomfortably on the floor.

'Stick together, that's what we'll do—it's the only way.' Horrendo wasn't listening to anything other than the wonderful idea that now gleamed behind his eyes. 'Let's wake up the boys and tell them,' he urged Rascal, hopping up and flexing his muscles under his shirt with enthusiasm.

'Curse a catfish,' exploded Rascal. 'Tell them *what*? How on earth will they escape from here, how will they survive in the water—?'

'I've got a *plan*, Rascal, we're going to *pull together*, listen—'

There was a loud snore as someone turned over, flinging his leg across another boy's face.

'Get off, fungus breath!' the boy mumbled.

'Pretty Pet,' Bombastic murmured in his sleep.

'They're not going to like it,' Rascal said gravely after he'd heard Horrendo's wild idea. 'You understand I'm only doing this because I trust you.'

At Rascal's words Horrendo stopped flexing and felt a familiar warm glow starting in his chest. It made the backs of his eyes tingle and his throat ache.

'That's *why* I'm doing this,' said Horrendo softly. 'Because everyone should have a chance to feel this . . . this throat ache. If Dogfish asked me now what's the point of a man's existence, I'd say—'

'You can explain that to the boys when they're in the middle of the ocean surrounded by white pointers. I'm sure it will cheer them up,' Rascal said dryly. 'Now you get going and I'll wake them all up.'

chapter ten

It was still dark when the Captain came striding towards the boys' cabin. From under half-closed lids Rascal watched him standing in the doorway, the pearly grey of dawn outlining his tall frame. Cussing catfish, why wasn't Horrendo back yet?

The Captain stood with his legs wide apart and his arms crossed. He peered around the room. Then with the suddenness of gunshot he bellowed, 'Get up you lazy louts, UP UP UP!'

Eyes flew open all around the room.

'Get moving! What have you got, lead in your pants? Up onto the deck NOW!'

The boys sprang into action and ran.

In five seconds flat they were all lined up along the starboard side of the ship.

Any minute now, thought Rascal, as he glanced at the row of anxious faces, and the Captain will notice one boy missing. The most important boy. The 'idiot'.

'Just a dash more wine to go with *you*,' Horrendo told the silent pink lobster sitting on the galley bench, 'and you can simmer lightly for an hour.'

Horrendo put the dish in the oven and glanced around with satisfaction. The benches gleamed with polish, the shelves were neatly stacked with supplies and a delicious meal was baking in the oven. (It was an act of kindness, Horrendo considered, to leave things nice for other people, especially when those other people didn't have a lot to look forward to.)

He smiled with a sudden thought and pulled out his pouch of herbs. Opening the oven door he sprinkled the last of the grains over the sizzling dish. 'A meal to remember,' he whispered to the lobster, and shut the door with a flourish.

'WHERE'S THAT IDIOT!'

The Captain's voice crashed through the galley from the deck. Horrendo jumped, straightening his back with a sudden crack. Wincing, he felt the pain shoot up between his shoulderblades. 'That jolly-boat was jolly heavy,' he muttered to himself as he flung out the door. 'And now I'm late. Oh, *why* do I always forget where I am when I'm cooking?'

He dashed up the steps and burst out into the rosy dawn. Squinting in the sudden light, it seemed amazing to him that only an hour ago he'd been labouring in the dark, alone at the stern, lowering the boat into the water. It had been hard work pulling on those ropes, yes sir! Shuddering, Horrendo saw a flash in his mind of the moment when he'd nearly dropped the ropes, just before the boat hit the water. 'But you'll never handle the boat on your own!' Rascal had wailed last night, and it was true that Horrendo's muscles like small hills had been stretched as never before. But all his swimming and lifting and carrying had served him well, and the crushing weight of the boat had eased slowly (and quietly) down to the water.

The pirates were stumbling onto the deck as Horrendo flung himself into line. His heart pounded with trepidation.

The men rubbed sleep from their eyes, leaning heavily against each other. The night before they'd handed around a couple of bottles of the Captain's rum that they kept stashed in the galley for emergencies. Dogfish had reckoned that Horrendo's imminent death should be considered such a crisis and they'd all agreed, so they'd fallen down unconscious in the small hours of the morning and luckily not heard the whining of the pulleys or the splash as Horrendo lowered the jolly-boat.

The Captain walked slowly along the line of boys, a whip in his hand. He looked into each face, his teeth bared in a sneer. 'Pack of dawdling dummies, aren't you?' he snarled. 'Lolling around, when there's work to be done. Well, things are going to change around here, mark my words.'

He stopped when he came to Horrendo. Lifting up his whip, he casually encircled it around Horrendo's neck and gave a sharp yank.

'Aaargh!' choked Horrendo.

'You'll be the first one to set an example, you sluggard!' he roared. 'Up to the plank with you, quick smart!'

The Captain pushed Horrendo towards the fo'c'sle deck where the wooden plank had been hauled out. Horrendo went skidding across the floor and fell over a rusty bucket full of greasy water. He crouched for a moment, clutching his bleeding knee.

'Walk!' hissed the Captain. 'And let this be a lesson to you all.'

Horrendo climbed the first step and looked back. He saw the pirates biting their lips. Most of them stared down at their feet. Dogfish gave a little wave but when the Captain swung around to see, he pretended he was scratching his head.

The boys trembled where they stood.

Horrendo took another step.

'Captain,' cried Dogfish suddenly, 'you can't—'

'Who dares to speak?' The look of thunder on the Captain's face made the pirates pale. 'Well?'

'It was Squid,' mumbled Dogfish.

'Was not!' cried Squid, punching him in the ribs. 'You lousy liar. Why, I'll—'

'March on, boy!' cried the Captain, and Horrendo stepped onto the plank.

The pirates all crept nearer to Horrendo, forming a tight, grieving circle. 'I wish I was still asleep and this was all a dream,' murmured Dogfish.

At a distance behind them, the boys shuffled nervously and looked to Rascal for the signal. Rascal clenched his teeth, waiting for the right moment.

'Captain sir,' piped up Horrendo, 'could I make a last request before I die?'

'No, jump, you donkey.'

There was a low rumble from the pirates, that began to grow like a swarming of bees. Their faces were reddening with anger, and some fingered their swords. For the first time the Captain looked uneasy.

'What is it then, vermin?'

Rascal was watching the men. When he saw that the Captain and crew were all concentrated on Horrendo, their backs to the boys, Rascal tapped his nose. Slowly, silently, the boys began to creep away.

They held their breath, inching along towards the stern, their eyes still on the pirates' backs.

Horrendo glanced over at the boys, quick as the flick of a fishtail. His stomach twisted with anxiety. It was going to take minutes for them to reach the side and slip over. Maybe it would only take seconds before someone discovered them escaping. He had to hold the men's attention . . .

'Well?' demanded the Captain. 'Get on with it!'

'I'm sorry,' said Horrendo. 'It's hard to get the words out when I'm feeling so . . . emotional.'

There was a loud sob, then a gulp as Dogfish tried to pretend he was coughing. Suddenly all the pirates were taken by fits of coughing, their shoulders shaking and their eyes streaming. 'Too right, aye aye,' muttered the men sympathetically.

'You see,' went on Horrendo, 'I wanted to ask if, when you go back for the boys next year, someone would be so kind as to tell my parents that I died bravely, doing my best.'

Dogfish let out a moan and his knees buckled under him.

The First Mate shot up his hand. 'I'll do that for you, matey!'

'Thank you,' said Horrendo. From the corner of his eye he saw that Mischief was first over the side.

'All right, boy,' roared the Captain. 'Jump!'

'There was just one other thing,' Horrendo put in frantically.

'*WHAT?!*'

'I'd like to give Mr Dogfish, sir, the recipe for my special lobster mornay before I leave this world.'

Mischief had gone, sliding down the rope and swinging into the jolly-boat that Horrendo had so carefully lowered in the dark.

As the Captain bellowed, 'Bloomin' *recipes* now!' and the men were protesting—'But lobster *mornay!*'— Horrendo saw Bombastic was next to disappear over the side.

'First you throw the lobster into boiling water,' Horrendo chanted loudly. 'Then, while it's cooking, you make a white sauce. Now, how does one go about making a white sauce, you may ask? Well...'

The boys followed Mischief and Bombastic and Hoodlum over the side, one by one, hands and feet clinging to the rope. Rascal went last, urging along Rip who was shaking so much that his sweaty hands nearly slid off the rope.

'Enough!' shouted the Captain when Horrendo was up to serving suggestions. 'Jump before I get out my sword and slice you up like a cucumber!'

A deep silence stole over the ship. It was like dusk falling, or a drifting shadow. The only sounds were the gentle caress of the sea against the sides and the occasional coughing of the pirates as they stood close together in the quiet of their thoughts.

Horrendo's stomach muscles tightened. All the boys were gone. He imagined them sitting still as stones, sweating with nerves as they waited for him in the boat below.

Taking his last look around the ship, at the pirates whose eyes were still moist, at the dreaded crow's nest and the black flag fluttering in the breeze, Horrendo leapt up in the air and bounced on the plank just as if it were a diving board. His body arched beautifully, turning in a somersault, and, as he dived down like a speeding bullet towards the fathomless sea, he took his deepest breath ever and yelled, 'Serve it hot, with just a sprinkle of black pepper!'

chapter Eleven

Down went Horrendo into folds of icy, heart-stopping water, down further until there was only darkness and the drum of his pulse. He kicked his legs and stretched out his arms, swimming deep under the ship. He had to make it to the other side where the jolly-boat waited, filled with boys. He could only guess how wide and deep the ship was, so he began to count the seconds to give himself a measure. After twenty his lungs felt like burst balloons. But all his breath-holding training at the bay came back to him. He fought down the panic and concentrated on his counting. He thought of nothing else—not the freezing water, not the flittering shapes of fish, nor the black shadow of the keel above him. Just twenty-one, twenty-two, twenty-three . . .

Meanwhile, the pirates had gathered at the side of the ship, peering down at the spot where Horrendo hit the water. They stared and stared, but there was no sign of the boy.

'Just like the old Blue Devil,' muttered Squid, wiping his eyes. 'Merciless sea just swallows 'em whole, pips an' all.'

'Nothing *like* the old Blue Devil,' spat Dogfish. 'He was special, our 'Orrendo, somethin' special.'

'At least yer've got yer lobster mornay,' said Wicked, smirking.

'Aye,' agreed the others.

'But it won't be the same without Horrendo cookin' it,' said the First Mate sadly.

Suddenly there was a bellow from the other side of the ship. 'Blasted sneaking vipers!' trumpeted the Captain. 'They're getting away!'

When the pirates rushed over, they saw Horrendo popping up out of the water like a champagne cork and springing into the boat. He took his place next to Rascal at the front, and the jolly-boat began hauling away, manned by nine grinning boys.

'Take that, sucker!' yelled Bombastic at the Captain.

'Drop dead, noodle brains!' shouted Demon.

The Captain stared, his steely mouth hanging loose and open for once in amazement. 'They've stolen the blathering jolly-boat! Can you believe it?'

Dogfish shook his head and turned away to hide his grin. He dug Squid in the ribs.

'Fire the cannons!' screamed the Captain.

'They're not on target, Cap'n,' growled the First Mate. 'By the time we've turned the ship about the boys will be out of range.'

'Ah, good riddance to you!' shouted the Captain in disgust. He shook his fist at the laughing boys. 'You'll rot out there like drowned kittens. Like dumped garbage. LIKE THE RUBBISH YOU ARE!'

Bombastic showed him the rude finger.

The distance was widening now between the boats but Horrendo heard the Captain say, 'It's not worth chasing those lag-eyed luggards. Let them perish and go to hell.'

Horrendo's heart did a leap of joy and he felt like bobbing up and doing a sailor's hornpipe, right there in the boat. He didn't, of course, just rowed extra hard and fast, calling to the boys, 'Turn on the speed and head for our new life of freedom!'

Perhaps it was this bold and rather overconfident statement that turned the boys surly. At Horrendo's words they all glanced back at the fast-disappearing speck of the pirate ship. On board the ship was, certainly, the mad, drink-sodden devil of a Captain they knew, but there was also food and water and shelter from the sun. Ahead to the east, where the sun was blooming now like a ripening strawberry, there was only the empty ocean of their future.

The boys scanned the horizon. No bump of land or ship interrupted the relentless straight line, as far as the eye could see. They gazed at an endless sea, an unknown universe, and shuddered deep in their souls.

'Fifteen miles, is it, to the nearest islands?' Rip whispered. He let go of his oars and cracked his knuckles.

'Big winds in store, eh?' muttered Demon, dropping his oars, too, and gazing at Horrendo.

'All in a jolly-boat that could break like a matchstick at the first hint of a gale?' growled Mischief. 'And me, I can only do dog paddle!'

The boys all let go of their oars and let the boat drift.

'Why did we let you talk us into this?' howled Demon, glancing from Rascal to Horrendo.

'Wasn't it worth it, but, to see the Captain's face?' yelped Hoodlum.

The boys grinned again for a moment, but then their faces paled as they stared out at the desolate sea.

'Me and Pest could have been having breakfast now,' growled Bombastic. 'You and yer schemes,' he went on, turning to Horrendo. 'Ya low-lying swamp weed, why did ya have ta go and change everything?'

He half stood up, leaning over Mischief and Demon, trying to get hold of Horrendo's neck. 'It's all your fault we're stuck out here in the middle of nowhere! I've got a good mind ta tip you out and leave ya gapin' like a fish, ta *swim* the fifteen miles!'

The boat tipped as Bombastic lunged at Horrendo. He lost his footing, sitting down suddenly on the hard wooden floor and cracking his knee.

'Stay in your places and listen,' Rascal hissed, 'or we'll all be tipped out like marbles. Now we gotta pull together, see? I *told* you about the Captain's plans for us—that ship of his'll be a floating coffin soon. None of us would have lasted the week. But there's no crow's nest to climb here nor sails to reef, and no Captain throwin' us to our deaths. This boat is sturdy, never you mind.'

The boys sat silently, their shoulders slumped in defeat.

Horrendo looked at them all, hunched side by side. He thought of his twelfth birthday and how they'd sat around his kitchen, gloomily planning their escapes. He remembered their voices of doom and the deathly pale of their faces. If only he could persuade them that this time it would be all right, that there was hope because they were all together. He watched Rip trying not to look down at the water, at Wildman biting the insides of his cheeks.

'Well, thank you, Rascal,' he began hesitantly. 'And I really do think we can succeed—we'll have an excellent journey, because we're all strong and hardy, and if we work as a team, you'll see we can cover this distance in no time. Ride the waves when they come—we'll fare better in this smaller vessel going *with* the sea than fighting it in that big ship.'

Bombastic snorted in disbelief, but said nothing. His hand went to the leather pouch where Pest lay sleeping. He gave the frog a quick pat through his waistcoat.

'Now, what we have to do, if you don't mind, is pull together in a fast and steady rhythm.' He grasped his oar. 'Count *one*, two, three as you ease back through the air. If we all pull at the same time, why, we'll fly along!'

'Sounds like a bloomin' waltz!' muttered Bombastic. In a high falsetto voice he sang, 'One, two, three, the owl and the nincompoop went to sea!'

Mischief, who sat next to him, giggled mournfully. No one else laughed, so he stopped and straightened his skinny shoulders. After a few seconds the boys, muttering into the air about how unfair life was and of all the crack-brained schemes they'd ever heard this took the lobster mornay, took up their oars and began to row.

On the count, they pulled through the water. There was silence as they heaved and hoed, Horrendo counting in rhythm above the hard breathing of the boys and the slap of the waves.

They headed east, towards the sun. After a short while they began to pick up speed. No one bothered to talk because it was heavy work and the count was

becoming hypnotic. It took all their concentration and they didn't think about monster winds or how hungry they were or how nitwitted Horrendo was bringing them here. Rowing *was* like dancing, Horrendo thought wildly—the strokes were like steps, everyone keeping in rhythm and doing their part. They were making something happen, all of them together, and now the boys were humming the count, their voices swelling and falling like the waves around them. Horrendo noticed the muscles of Bombastic's back clenching and relaxing, tightening and loosening in just the right rhythm. It looked like a happy back, Horrendo ventured to think, and he smiled a small private smile of hope.

The jolly-boat thrust its way through the water, the gulls swooping overhead. The morning air was bright and shiny, and Horrendo was sure they must have done seven or eight miles already.

The boys had little pauses every now and then, for their muscles and hands ached after a while, and they took it in turns to row and rest. Horrendo tried to keep his eyes pinned on the sea ahead, looking out for a shadow or the shape of an island. It would be easy to miss a small patch of land in all that vast ocean, and Horrendo wished for the hundredth time that he had a telescope.

And then, as he stared out at sea, on the third stroke of his oar, he saw something. He stopped rowing and peered at the black triangle sticking out of the water. It was moving at a powerful rate, slicing through the sea towards them. Oh please, oh please, don't let it be a fin, he thought feverishly, don't let it be *that*. He remembered stories of great monster sharks encircling boats, turning them over just like pieces of toast, and devouring men, bones, oars and all.

He watched the black triangle coming nearer and terror seared through him, burning his lungs. He tried to call out, but his throat wouldn't work. For a second he closed his eyes. He realised then that the dread he'd felt before in his life—pirates, plank-walking, the Captain's eyes—was nothing, just a crumb, a dust-speck of horror compared to this.

Mischief, who was sitting up front, saw the fin too. 'Shark!' he yelled, his voice breaking into a scream. 'Shark, shark, *shark*!'

Rip and Hoodlum both dropped their oars and froze.

'Shout!' yelled Rascal. 'Shout like crazy! Pick up your oars and splash the water, make an infernal noise!'

But the boys sat still as pieces of wood, as if a spell had been put on them.

'Shouldn't we pretend to be dead,' whispered Wildman, 'you know, just a floating shipwreck with no tasty bits?'

'No,' shouted Rascal. 'Do as I tell you—I read all about it in Petrifying Pets.'

'I can't watch!' cried Rip, who was dying to crack his knuckles but couldn't on account of his hand being grabbed by Mischief.

'We're dead meat,' whimpered Hoodlum. 'We might as well be lying on a plate with mushrooms.'

'Bottom-dwelling swill-sucker, take that!' roared Bombastic, pounding the water with his oar. He leaned over and grabbed Demon's oar as well, crashing and splashing at the water, swearing and puffing and yelling insults at everything. The other boys unfroze too and yelled and bashed with him.

But more sharks were coming. Six, seven, a whole pack of them. The distance between the boys and the sharks shrank and soon they could see the great grey shadows of their bodies just under the water.

Horrendo could say nothing. He tried to yell, too, but no words came out. In that split second, as he looked at the boys, he blinked and saw a bunch of skeletons dancing on the bottom of the ocean. Soon they'd be still, their small white bones picked over by the little fish swimming by.

And it was all his fault.

All of it.

A grey sleek body leapt out of the water, just near the boat, and the boys screamed. They caught the flash of a cheeky grin and a croaky laugh before it dived down again like an acrobat.

So filled with visions of doom was Horrendo, that he didn't notice for a moment that Rascal had stopped yelling and splashing. He was sitting in his place, hands bunched on his knees, a huge grin spreading across his face.

Horrendo grieved for his friend who'd lost his mind to terror.

Then Rascal pointed at the water. 'Look, you great ninny, dolphins!'

'Dolphins?' echoed Horrendo, and such a tide of relief washed over him that he felt dizzy. 'Dolphins!' he laughed. 'Dolphins!'

'Is that all right then?' whispered Rip, bending his thumb back till it cracked.

'Sure is,' yelled Rascal and dived over the side, quick as lightning. He hurtled towards the dolphins, making strange squeaky sounds and little croaky laughs.

The boys watched in amazement as Rascal grabbed one of the dolphin fins, swooping down under the surface and up again, playing as he had in the bay back home.

Rip looked at him in admiration. 'Never knew Rascal could swim like that,' he said. 'D'ya see how friendly they are? They're a good luck sign, I reckon.'

'Fool notion,' growled Bombastic. But as he looked

out at the frolicking dolphins, the smile on his face was something the boys had never seen before.

Rascal swam back to the boat and climbed to his place. The dolphins came squeaking and chattering around the boat, leaping out of the water and taking off again in a whoosh of white. They swam off and circled back, swooping away and coming nearer until Rascal slapped his knee and cried, 'Sizzling swordfish, they're trying to tell us something!'

Horrendo nodded in excitement. 'They're showing us the way to the islands, don't you think? They want to save us!'

'Piffle shmiffle!' sniffed Mischief, glancing at Bombastic.

But Bombastic was too busy getting his oar into place and watching the dolphins. 'So what are we waiting for?' he shouted, and began to pull.

'One, two, three!' cried Horrendo, his heart leaping just like the dolphins.

'What about those monster winds round the islands, but?' whispered Rip to Hoodlum next to him. But Hoodlum didn't hear over the counting and the humming and the excitement, which was probably just as well.

After an hour or so, with the dolphins swimming ahead and circling back, Horrendo spied a dark-green patch of land. From the distance it seemed to float on the water, flat and furry, like someone's forgotten wig. But the dolphins guided them past the island and on into the open sea.

Now a wind sprang up, whipping the waves into spray. The boys could feel the current quickening as they dragged their oars through the sea.

'We should've stopped at that first bit of land!' yelled Mischief over the wind.

'We have to trust the dolphins!' Horrendo yelled back. But his heart was quaking inside him.

The sky clouded over. The boys had been riding along a gilded sea but now shadows lurked in the little valleys of the breaking waves.

'Hold tight to your oars, boys,' Horrendo called.

As they rowed into the darkening air, the wind stung their skins, sending up waves that rose like hills before them. The jolly-boat sailed over small cliffs, sliding down the belly of waves with crashing force. Rip closed his eyes and began to pray.

When the next wave rose and they had a view for a moment, the boys caught a glimpse of a towering black headland reaching out towards them. The dolphins headed through a narrow channel of sea, bordered by a string of spiky rocks. Still following the dolphins, the boys steered the boat towards the mouth of the channel, but they were yelling with fear.

'We're gonna crash on those *rocks*!' shouted Mischief, closing his eyes.

But as they entered the channel the wind dropped, and the waves were no longer cliffs, just little choppy parts of a quietening stretch of water. And when Mischief opened his eyes he saw why the boys were all cheering like thunder. At the end of the channel a sheltered beach lay like a gift, as magnificent and inviting as paradise.

chapter twelve

The boys woke in the dappled shade of coconut palms. They blinked and yawned, looking out at the golden rind of beach that lay before them. Waves frilled neatly onto the shore. Behind them a hill furred with trees sang with the chatter of birds and monkeys.

'How lucky we are!' gasped Horrendo.

'What'll we eat?' asked Rip.

'What'll we drink?' demanded Rowdy.

'Let's explore,' said Bombastic, sitting up. 'I'm ready for tigers and lions.' He made a fist, then winced. 'Just as soon as I've had another lie-down.'

The boys stretched out on the sand and massaged their aching limbs. They'd been asleep for a whole afternoon and night.

After they'd waved goodbye to the dolphins the day before, they'd dragged the heavy jolly-boat up onto the shore. But as soon as their feet touched dry sand, all the terror, relief and rowing suddenly drained them like rum sucked from a bottle, and they'd fallen asleep where they dropped. The sun sank as they snored, sending flames over the sea, and the moon rose trailing silver, but the boys had dreamed on through the night.

'If you give me a leg up, Rascal,' Horrendo said now, yawning, 'I'll try to climb this palm tree and get us a coconut or two.'

The boys eyed the tall trees with suspicion. There were no branches for footholds, and the trunk seemed to go on forever.

'Why don't you just shake 'em down?' suggested Rowdy.

'I can do that!' agreed Bombastic enthusiastically. He stood up, groaning a little with stiffness, then bounced over to the nearest tree. Before Horrendo had time to say anything, Bombastic had given the trunk a hefty shove with his whole body and a ripe coconut fell, hitting Wildman on the head.

'What the—?' Wildman exploded. 'As if I 'aven't suffered enough what with cruel captains and witherin' winds, and now I go and get a coconut dropped on my head like a bloomin' cannon!'

He sat up, rubbing his forehead. From the ocean came a loud croaky laugh and the boys looked up to see a dolphin leaping over the waves.

They grinned and broke into soft chuckles.

'Those animals are a lot smarter than some *boys* I know,' remarked Bombastic, gazing fondly out at the water.

'Angels of the sea,' remarked Rip poetically.

'That's dolphins for you,' said Rascal.

Horrendo got up and began to bash the coconut against a tree to crack its hard shell. More coconuts fell and soon the boys were sitting around eating the delicious white meat and slurping coconut juice.

'This is the life,' murmured Rip.

'Aye,' agreed Mischief. 'No one tellin' us what to do.'

'No slavin' away on deck.'

'No whippin' or kickin' in the ribs.'

'No climbin' the blasted crow's nest.'

'No insults or rude remarks,' finished Horrendo with a glad sigh.

The boys looked at him.

'Hmm,' they said and went on eating the coconut.

In a little while, when the sound of smacking lips and idle talk had quietened, and the boys were lying down in the shade, an uneasy silence fell. In the heat of the morning even the monkeys were still.

'It's unnatural, this quiet, ain't it?' said Rip nervously.

'Quiet as a tomb, maybe,' replied Mischief. He looked out at the empty sea. 'I mean, what if we're buried alive here? It's all very well for a day, but we can't go on livin' on coconuts forever, can we?'

The boys were silent again, thinking.

'What'll we do if the pirate ship comes?' asked Rip.

'What'll we do if no pirate ship comes?' asked Mischief.

Rip cracked his knuckles. It sounded like gunshot in the stillness.

Bombastic jumped. 'Will you *stop* doing that? Gives me the willies, you nervous little ninnyhammer!'

'Now, now,' said Horrendo. 'If you don't mind me saying so, the dolphins didn't save our lives only for us to bicker them away. The thing to do is to make a plan.'

Just then Rascal leapt up as if a snake had bitten him. 'There!' he cried, pointing towards the horizon. 'A ship on the horizon!'

The boys squinted into the sun.

'Oh, viper-vomit,' moaned Rowdy, 'I couldn't bear to look at that devil of a Captain again.'

'Or feel his whip on yer back,' said Mischief feelingly.

'Or hear his curses in yer ears,' said Rip softly.

Horrendo said nothing. He turned away, his shoulders dropping. Could it be that this great journey, this courageous escape into freedom, had all been for nothing? Would they have to turn around and go back as prisoners to that floating gaol?

'We don't know it's them,' Rascal said to him hopefully. 'It may be a good ship come to rescue us.'

'Aw, in yer dreams, Rascal,' said Bombastic, clenching his fists.

Horrendo thought of the Captain's pitiless shark eyes, and shivered.

The boys said nothing more. They just waited together, there on the sand, staring out at the horizon. And sure enough, as the ship drifted closer, they recognised the carved figurehead of the cobra at the bow, the black flag streaming from the mast.

'We must hide,' said Horrendo urgently. 'That's something I'm good at.'

'Where?' The boys gazed at him fearfully.

'Follow me.' Horrendo set off into the forest, picking his way through vines as solid as his wrist, stepping over tangled roots and fallen branches. Presently he found a clump of bushes so thick and intertwined that the boys could arrange themselves behind them and still spy through the leaves.

Wildman grunted. 'And what'll we do if they find us? We ain't got no weapons!'

'I've still got Pet here, I mean Pest,' said Bombastic.

Wildman grunted. 'Pest would probably love them to death, he's so sozzled.'

Bombastic went to clout him but Rascal cut in. 'There might only be a few pirates left,' he said. 'It's amazing they got through that strait at all without losing every one.'

'Yes, but you can be sure the Captain will be

amongst those remainin', and no mistake,' replied
Wildman gloomily.

'We'll ambush them!' hissed Bombastic. 'See,
that way we'll have the advantage of surprise. We'll
climb the trees, and soon as they come crashin'
through here, we'll jump on 'em and wring their necks
for 'em!'

'Oh aye, just like you jumped on the Blue Devils
and beat them all to a pulp, eh?' jeered Wildman.

'Well, 'ave you got a better idea, fathead?'

'Ssh, ssh, please,' whispered Horrendo. 'For Plan A,
let's just hide here for now, and for Plan B we'll carry
out Bombastic's strategy if necessary.'

Bombastic nodded and puffed out his chest.

The boys crouched among the prickly grasses and
sticks for over an hour. While they waited in silence,
trying not to fidget, with Mischief holding Rip's
knuckles tightly in his so he wouldn't crack them,
Horrendo couldn't help thinking how changed the
boys seemed. They were pulling together. That's what
was different. They were working as a team. The
thought of this made him feel such a glow of warmth
and pride that it calmed his pounding heart and filled
the empty quiet. Only the nagging little voice at the
back of his head kept asking questions. 'What will we
all do alone on the island? When will we see our
families again? What if someone's appendix bursts?
What if Rascal gets a cold? What if coconuts are not
enough for boys to live on?'

Bombastic was just about to stand up for a stretch,

already flexing his knees, when they heard a muffled curse and a branch snap.

Horrendo put his finger to his lips. The boys held their breath.

A pirate stepped out from the trees. He burped loudly and clutched his belly. Sitting down suddenly on a fallen log, he mopped his brow.

'Stinkin' stomach will be the death of me,' he muttered.

'Aye, and it's as hot as a witch's cauldron,' said another, stepping up and joining him on the log. 'Feel the heat more now, I do, since me poor earlobe's no longer with me.'

'What's that got to do with it?' said the first pirate.

'Well, I been thinkin', and I reckon the earlobe must be some kinda coolin' agent, see? That's its function.'

'Hmm,' said the first, scratching his chin. 'I can see yer point an' all. When you've got long ones like mine, they kinda flap in the breeze and fan ya.'

'Aye,' replied the other. 'But there's no need to show off about it.'

'Wasn't,' said the first pirate, and he burped again.

'Was,' said the second.

Horrendo knew that burp anywhere. He wondered how Dogfish's indigestion was faring, without a ration of Mother's home remedy.

There was a loud crashing of branches and stamping through the undergrowth and another pirate clambered up. Horrendo made a gap in the bushes, poking at the

web of little branches with his index finger. His eye at
the hole, he saw the First Mate standing with his
hands on his hips, towering over the other two men.

The pirates looked in bad shape. Dogfish had a gash
down his neck and shoulder, which was sticky with
dried blood. He slapped lazily at the flies clustered
around it. Buzzard slumped on the log, drawing
something in the dirt with his big toe.

The First Mate stared down at them, scowling. His
bushy beard was straggly and stuck together in clumps
with tiny crumbs of fish bone and some kind of
greyish sauce. When he shook his head, as he did now,
little bits of dinner flew off and scattered over the

pirates. They didn't bother to wipe them off, just sat there slapping miserably at the flies.

'What are ya doin', sittin' down on the job, mateys?' boomed the First Mate. He drew out a piece of parchment from his waistband and laid it flat on the ground. Horrendo had a quick glimpse of a map and a drawing of a box all etched around in gold exclamation marks. Treasure!

'Now don't go gettin' bossy like you-know-who,' said Dogfish, killing a fly and inspecting it on his palm.

'Aye,' agreed Buzzard. 'You know what happens to bossy boots,' and he drew a finger across his throat, grinning evilly.

'Let's find this gold, mateys,' said the First Mate, picking at his beard, 'and we can all—'

Just then Bombastic, who had been spying through the bushes, leant forward too far to see the map and pricked his eye with a twig. '*Ouch!*' he cried, and, too late, slapped his hand over his mouth.

'Idiot!' hissed Demon.

'What was that?' whispered the First Mate.

'Natives?' suggested Dogfish.

'Get yer swords ready!' said the First Mate.

Cautiously he took a step forward and swiped at the bushes with his sword.

'Hey, look out, you great goon!' yelled Mischief who'd almost been stabbed in the chest.

The pirates loomed over the bushes and stared at the boys huddled there. Horrendo stood up shyly and put out his hand.

'It's really nice to see you again, really very nice,' he said. 'But I must say you men don't look at all well. That cut is nasty, Mr Dogfish, and if you don't mind me saying so it needs tending.'

The men goggled at Horrendo and his outstretched hand, their mouths open. Then the First Mate broke into a grin.

'And it's bloomin' marvellous to see *you* again, matey,' he cried, pumping Horrendo's hand up and down with all his might. 'See 'ow skinny I've got without you on board?' And he clapped his huge belly that hung over his pants, making it wobble like a jelly.

The other boys stood up now and shook hands with the pirates and grinned. Bombastic broke a couple of thick branches on his knees in his excitement. Maybe they wouldn't have to eat coconuts for the rest of their lives . . .

But Rascal stepped into the group and said quietly, 'Where is the Captain? Could you hide us somewhere? He'll surely kill us as soon as he sees us!'

The First Mate looked back at Dogfish and Buzzard. They exchanged sly smiles and clapped each other on the back.

'Aye,' said the First Mate, 'it's a long story. See—'

'Let *me* tell it,' cried Dogfish, settling himself on the log again.

'No, *me*,' put in Buzzard. 'I'm the one who lost an ear.'

'Oh, you and yer confounded ear,' groaned Dogfish. 'Are we ever goin' to *'ear* the end of it. Ha haaa . . .'

'You shouldn't laugh at other people's misfortunes.'

'Will you just tell us where the Captain is?' blurted Rascal.

'Well,' said the First Mate, as they all sat down on the grassy ground. 'It was like this. After you walked the plank, 'Orrendo—aye, that was something, eh? We was all in shock, like, we couldn't believe it. How did you swim right under the ship, boy?'

'And how did you all get 'ere in those *winds*?' asked Buzzard.

'That's a long story,' said Horrendo. 'But please, you go first, if you don't mind.'

'Aye,' said the First Mate. 'See what pretty manners he has, mateys? Can't you copy 'em and be civil? Anyway, there we all was, standin' on the deck with our mouths hangin' open—'

'When the Captain says, "Good riddance to bad rubbish!"' put in Mischief.

'Aye, he's got no heart, that one,' said the First Mate.

'Made of wood,' said Dogfish.

'Tin,' said Buzzard.

'Shark cartilage,' suggested Rip.

'Aye,' agreed the First Mate, 'and then he turns to us and says, "We're goin' through the Scorpio Straits," and Dogfish here has to go and climb the mast and reef the sails.'

'Aye, with my stomach an' all!' shuddered Dogfish.

'And I say to the Captain, Captain, I says, we don't have to go right through the strait, we can *avoid* it, see? If we sailed south and looped around the islands, we'd enter safely. Go around them, like. It'd only take an extra day or two, with favourable winds. But the Captain got out his whip and cracked it and told me to shut me gob or he'd throw me overboard like a left-over dinner, so impatient he was.

'And sure enough, as we approached the straits the sea grew dark and choppy and the swell turned into huge waves that just kept thunderin' and crashin' all over the deck, and still the Captain yelled at the crew to stop clingin' to the sides and slosh out the water and keep reefin' the sails. When any second we'd be sloshed out of the ship like sardines ourselves if we didn't hang on! And then suddenly, you know what? I thought, what's the point?'

'Aye,' nodded Dogfish, 'what's the blasted point of it all?'

'There I was,' went on the First Mate, 'about to die in the next five minutes, and what joy 'ave I 'ad in me miserable life? What blessed second of happiness?'

'We had swordfish soup, but,' Dogfish reminded him.

'One lousy pot of swordfish soup in all our years at sea. Why should we die, I says to meself, why *should* we, just for this mangy old coot with a heart of wood?'

'Tin,' said Buzzard.

'Shark cartilage,' said Rip.

'So you know what we did?' the First Mate cut in.

'What?' cried Horrendo and the boys together.

'We got a rope and, Dogfish and me, we crept up behind the Captain while he was bellowin' at the men and we jumped 'im. We tied him to the mast while old Goosey got the little dinghy ready.'

'No!' cried Horrendo.

'Yes, yes!' shouted Bombastic and the boys.

'Aye,' nodded the First Mate. 'And then we tossed 'im over the side into the boat with a bottle of his favourite rum. "Good riddance," we says, "the drink's on us!"'

There was silence for a moment and a monkey hooted overhead.

'Blimey,' whispered Rascal. 'That's mutiny.'

The First Mate thrust out his chin. 'It was him or us. He would have murdered the lot of us if we hadn't got rid of 'im. And then we turned right around before the winds got any worse and went the long way.'

The pirates were quiet, remembering the sight of their Captain bobbing over the waves until the distance and the monster waves swallowed him up.

'Do you think we'll still get into heaven, but?' asked Buzzard hesitantly.

Suddenly there was a snapping of branches nearby and Goose and Squid broke through, followed by four more pirates.

'Well, look who we have here,' cried Squid. 'The lobster king!'

'How did you make it, boys?' asked a pirate called Scabrous, shaking hands.

And so Horrendo began the tale, assisted by Rascal and Bombastic, Demon and Wildman, Mischief and Hoodlum, while Rowdy cracked open more coconuts for the pirates and Rip cracked his knuckles.

'So, we're lookin' for the Blue Devil treasure,' said the First Mate at last.

Up in the trees a monkey suddenly screamed. The branches swayed dangerously low as monkeys swiped at each other, fighting for fruit. The noise was deafening until a furry body fell out of the tree and landed like a bomb near the men's feet.

The First Mate jumped, startled. Then he straightened his shoulders (as if he'd just been having a good stretch) and pulled at his beard, spraying the men around him with coconut milk. 'Let's start lookin' now, mateys, or it'll be nightfall before we know it.' He

glanced up at the trees and added, 'Watch out for them mean monkeys as we go.'

Bombastic squared his jaw. 'If we help you search for the treasure, do we get a share?'

There was quiet for a moment as the men pondered.

'Fair's fair,' said Dogfish softly.

'Aye,' agreed Goose.

'Depends how much there is, but,' said Wicked, scratching a mosquito bite on his chin.

'All right, all right,' sighed the First Mate. 'Let's just find the blasted loot first and then we'll worry about sharing it.' He smoothed out the map on the ground before him and the pirates and boys all clustered around breathing heavily over each other's shoulders.

'Pew! What did you have for breakfast, Dogfish, you smell like a wart-hog's behind!'

'And you pong like mouldy pig droppings.'

'If I might interrupt,' Horrendo put in politely, 'I think you should follow this path through the forest. See, it goes straight up the mountain. I glimpsed a clearing in that direction when we were looking for somewhere to hide, and look, the map shows a kind of track leading up to a hut.'

The pirates looked where Horrendo was pointing. A picture of a hut was drawn around the treasure box all etched in golden exclamation marks, and a devil's head showed on the door.

'Aye,' agreed the First Mate. 'Show us the path, boy!' he cried and, after carefully stashing the map back in his waistband, he rubbed his hands with glee.

chapter thirteen

With a burning sun on their necks, pirates and boys
trudged along a rough path heading up the mountain.
The track was steep and uneven, with tree roots criss-
crossing over the ground and vines dangling in their
way. The First Mate took the lead as the jungle

thickened, hacking at the vines and branches before
them. It was hot, thirsty work, and the pirates hadn't
thought to bring water.

'I don't know about youse,' panted Buzzard, 'but
I'm sweatin' like an old cheese.'

'Aye,' nodded Goose, 'and me throat's as dry as a
ship's biscuit.'

The First Mate stopped suddenly and wiped his forehead with the back of his hand. The men looked up at the mountain. It seemed as if they were still at the bottom.

The First Mate drew out the map again. 'That hut carved with the devil's sign doesn't look so far up the mountain. How come we haven't seen it yet?'

'May I have a look at the map, please?' asked Horrendo. The boys gathered around as he pored over the parchment. 'How fascinating! This is a volcanic island, you know.'

Rip cracked his knuckles. 'Still active, does it say?' he asked nervously.

'No,' replied Horrendo. 'I mean, it doesn't say. But I would think the hut is somewhere near, to the west of this path. Mr First Mate, sir, did you bring your telescope?'

'Oh aye,' he said, drawing it out. 'Now there's an idea.' He put it to his eye. 'To the west, eh?' and suddenly he sprang into the air. 'I can see it, I spotted it, it's there! Only an hour's walk, I reckon. Hurray! Fandoodle! Pickle me toes and pour rum up me nose, we've made it!'

The pirates flung their arms around each other and did a wild jig right there on the stony path.

'Ouch, flamin' pebbles! Ger'off, Goose!' yelled Dogfish.

The First Mate flung ahead now at a cracking pace, veering west off the path, hacking away with his cutlass at the vegetation. Every now and then he climbed a tree and took out his telescope to check the hut's direction. Then he'd scramble down again, cutting and swiping at the vines. Pirates and boys hurtled after him, their thirst forgotten.

Now they entered a small clearing, and there before them stood a shaky hut, built with coconut palms. But as they drew closer they heard a loud screaming coming from inside the hut.

'Someone's got there first!' cried Bombastic.

'Pirates!' whispered Hoodlum.

'Blue Devils,' hissed Squid.

The First Mate motioned for them to stay where they were. He crept forward. Slowly, gripping his sword tightly, he inched towards the door of the hut. It was just slightly ajar and, taking a deep breath, he put his eye to the opening.

Suddenly the door was flung open and the First Mate leapt back, a look of horror frozen on his face.

'Aaargh!' he yelled, as a mass of hooting smelly bodies shot towards him. He started to run backwards, tripping over roots and stones. 'Baboons!' he cried. 'Great red-bottomed baboons. Yellow teeth like bulls' horns! Oh, sizzling stonefish, what'll we do?'

No one had time to give any advice as the baboons came galloping out of the hut, hooting and chattering.

The leader had a bunch of bananas in his mouth and the others came after him, furious. Rip was knocked flat as they streamed past the pirates like a rushing river and poured down the mountain.

Gingerly, the boys followed the pirates into the hut.

'Pew!' breathed Squid. 'This place smells worse than a Dogfish burp.'

The ground was covered with baboon droppings and there were no windows.

'Open the door wider!' yelled the First Mate.

The sunlight revealed an old box in the corner, the wood silvered with time.

'Look, our fortune, the answer to our old age!' cried Squid, rushing forward.

'Steady on,' the First Mate said, his sword raised. 'Let's do things in an orderly fashion,' and he ran to be first to tear open the box.

As the pirates fell over one another to see, the First Mate worked at the rusty lock with his sword. Sweat dripped from his forehead.

'Flamin' stubborn lock!' he cursed.

Then the lid flew open.

The pirates gasped. They were too shocked to swear.

The box was empty.

The First Mate lifted it up and shook it upside down. Not even a beetle fell out. The silence throbbed inside the hut. The men's devastated breathing was the only sound. The First Mate hurled the box across the floor and threw himself down on the ground, oblivious to the baboon droppings.

'Festerin' old devil!' he sobbed, pounding the earth with his fists. 'It was all a trick, a devilish trick. Oh it's not fair, not fair, not *fair*!' And he collapsed on his great stomach and wept into the earth.

All around him, the pirates began to curse and cry. The boys looked at each other in alarm as the pirates' rage boiled over. Kicking walls and throwing handfuls of dirt, they lunged at each other's chests. But then Rascal spied, in amongst the wave of movement and sound, one point of stillness in the hut.

Horrendo.

He was crouched over the flat square of earth where the treasure box had been, studying the soil. To Rascal he seemed like the eye of a hurricane, still, transfixed, completely unmoved by the writhing winds of agony around him. He'd discovered something, Rascal was sure of it, and as he crept nearer to see, he felt he was being drawn into a secret centre of energy.

The First Mate must have sensed something similar, for in a few seconds he sat up and looked over at Horrendo. His eyes narrowed in suspicion as he watched the boy. 'What are you lookin' at?' he growled.

Horrendo didn't answer straightaway. He was digging up handfuls of soil where the treasure chest had lain and gazing at it thoughtfully.

'Well?' the First Mate demanded. 'Catfish got yer tongue?'

Horrendo looked up from the ground. 'Sir, I think I know where the treasure is.'

The pirates stopped lunging and kicking.

'Where? Where?' they shouted, crowding around.

'Get back, give him some air!' cried Rascal, fending them off.

'The boy's right,' said the First Mate, standing in front of Horrendo protectively as if *he* were the treasure. 'Now, let's 'ave some quiet and hear what our dear 'Orrendo has to say.' He was rubbing his hands again in anticipation and except for his red eyes you'd never know he'd been weeping only seconds before.

Horrendo looked at the First Mate. He studied the pirates' faces. 'If I tell you all the exact location of the treasure—'

'If? *If?!*'

'Quiet please, everyone. If I tell you, will you please promise that you'll share the treasure with us boys?'

There was a hum of eager voices. 'Aye aye, of course, no problem there, only fair—'

'Aye, we'll share all right,' the First Mate boomed over everyone. 'You can be sure of that!'

'Do I have your word? *All* of you?'

The pirates solemnly put their hands on their hearts, every one of them.

'Well, if you'll look here at this soil,' Horrendo went on, 'you'll see that it is quite a different colour from the earth surrounding it.'

'Oh aye, darker, isn't it,' murmured the pirates, 'now that you come to think about it?'

'Aye, it's more coarse, like.'

Horrendo started to dig. 'The treasure has been buried under this spot, I think. That box was just a decoy.'

'I *said* it was a trick, didn't I!' roared the First Mate and he flung himself down next to Horrendo and began to dig. Soil flew over his shoulders, spraying the pirates behind him. Horrendo sat back on his heels as the digging went deeper and deeper.

And then, with a shout of triumph, the First Mate reached into the hole and pulled out a leather bag. He tipped it up and fistfulls of gold coins tumbled out.

'Pickle me piles,' he cried, jumping up with joy and throwing the bag into the air, 'there's a hundred of em down there!'

But before he could reach back in, the pirate Wicked shoved past, knocking him over and reaching his hands right into the hole. Laughing like a mad hyena, he scooped up bags of gold, stuffing them down his pants, in his shirt, his pockets and up his headscarf. Springing away with his back to the doorway, he unsheathed his sword and pointed it at the boys.

'This is pirate gold,' he cried, grinning and gloating so that all his black teeth showed. 'Pirate gold, d'ya hear? We earned every gold coin, eh, mateys?' He flashed a burning glance at the pirates. 'All those battles, those terrible, starvin' years. Now we can retire and rest up a bit, eh?'

Wicked kept looking wildly round the room, trying to catch the pirates' eyes. Dogfish looked down at his toes. There was complete quiet in the hut. The boys

held their breath. Bombastic clenched his fists. The only movement was the pirate Scabrous, who was inching his way past the boys to join Wicked, looking innocently all around him as if he just couldn't help what his feet were doing.

Horrendo stepped forward. 'But you promised, sir,' he said softly to Wicked.

'Did I?' replied Wicked with an evil grin. 'D'ya know, I've got the most dastardly memory. Must be the rum what's killin' me brain. Eh, fellas,' he asked the pirates, 'has the rum sizzled yer brains too?'

Silence. Squid cleared his throat. The First Mate clutched his leather bag.

'You *promised*,' Horrendo said again quietly.

'I told ya already,' spat Wicked, his voice rising, 'we earned it after twenty years at sea. Your time'll come, you'll see. Meanwhile, go stick yer head up a rat's bum.'

And I hope your brain shrivels to the size of a mouse dropping, thought Horrendo furiously, and all your rotten teeth fall from your gums and choke you, you miserable lying cheat. But, 'Very well, then,' he said. 'Please take the gold as a reward for all your hard work and I'm sure you'll make good use of it.'

Wicked grinned boldly at the boys who sent up a howl of protest. As Horrendo turned sadly away, doomed forever to be his Charming self, Rascal jumped out and faced the pirates.

'That's our gold too, and you know it,' he said loudly. 'You wouldn't have found it if we hadn't helped you.' He drew a deep breath, about to go on, but was distracted by a movement behind the pirates. Out of the corner of his eye, Rascal spied Bombastic slowly edging away from the group, making towards the door, with Pest peeping out of his pocket.

The pirates shuffled uncomfortably, still looking at Rascal.

'Yeah,' said Rip, stumbling forward into the gap. He cracked his knuckles nervously in the quiet. 'It was Horrendo here who showed you a different way to live. He...er...reminded all of us that life could be good. Why, if it hadn't been for him, you'd be still following

Captain's orders, never knowin' any better. You'd be lyin' right now at the bottom of the sea, yer bones tossed about by the killin' currents of the Scorpio Strait.'

The pirates pulled at their ears (those who had them) and scratched their chins in embarrassment.

'It's true,' whispered Dogfish, nodding at the First Mate.

But before they had time to reply, there was a loud, heart-stopping crash near the doorway. Wicked fell forward onto his face with Bombastic on his back like a gigantic tick. 'Die, ya thievin' double-crosser!' he bellowed. Pest glowed like fire on his shoulder, glaring dangerously at Wicked.

'Fantastic lunge, Bomberman!' shouted Mischief and, quick as a blink, he grabbed the sword that had fallen out of Wicked's hand. Pulling the pirate up by the collar, he held the sharp point to the pirate's throat.

'Great sword play, Mischief,' yelled Bombastic, and clapped him heartily on the back. 'Good Pet,' he added softly, opening his pocket for the loyal frog to hop back into.

'Wonderful team work all round!' cried Horrendo, beaming from one to the other as if his face would split.

The boys crowded in, pulling bags of gold out of Wicked's pants and exclaiming and miming Bombastic's lunge. They hooted with joy as the pirates coughed and cleared their throats, mumbling about how of

course they were going to share and what did the boys take them for and look at that Wicked, wasn't he a one, always thinkin' of himself like the selfish old dog that he was, but won't they teach 'im a trick or two by Jove, see if they don't.

The air was darkening and the forest had turned inky as Horrendo stepped out of the hut. He looked up beyond the black line of trees and saw a scarlet sky. To the west, clouds were outlined in brilliant rose and yellow—didn't they look like battleships burning in a sea of gold? How marvellous!

'Come and see this!' he called, bouncing up and down on his heels with pleasure. 'There's more treasure out here than all the gold on earth!'

Hearing the word 'treasure' the men tumbled out in a rush, bumping into Horrendo like a pack of dominoes. Their hopeful gaze followed his, but after a dumbfounded moment they sighed heavily. ('Just a damn fool sunset,' hissed Scabrous from the back.)

Horrendo, thinking the men were gasping in delight, smiled. Weren't they standing shoulder to shoulder, united in this moment of peace and beauty? He felt a great contentment. This isn't just surviving, he thought, gazing at the glowing sky, this is *living*. At last.

He was wondering if it might not be the very moment to ask the men to all join hands and lift their voices in a song of rejoicing, when a wailing sound rushed through the air like a whip, and five pirates crashed to the ground behind him. Like felled trees another five went down and another—it was happening so quickly that Horrendo couldn't make out what disaster had befallen them until he too felt something grab his chest and pull tight, and he slumped to the forest floor with the rest of them.

Panting heavily, the boys and men looked up to see a tall figure towering above. He stood silhouetted against the sky like a pillar of stone, his features hard to distinguish. But as they stared and shifted under their ropes, a growing terror dried the very spittle in their mouths.

'Lassoed like a bunch of cattle,' sneered the figure. 'Incompetent ninnies! IDIOTS!' His voice was rusty, hardly human, nails scraping on a tin roof. But the men would have known that voice anywhere. Anywhere.

'It can't be!' moaned Buzzard.

'Tell me I'm dreaming!' whispered Dogfish.

'It ain't natural,' groaned Goose.

'He's *super*natural,' nodded Squid. 'I always thunk it.'

Horrendo stared up at the Captain and a cold, ghostly finger inched along his spine. He shivered, his top lip suddenly damp. As he struggled, trying to stand, the rope tightened and he fell back.

The Captain laughed. All the men winced at the sound of it. A thin whistle like the wind off the arctic sea whined through his teeth, and not a muscle moved on his face. As he stepped nearer they saw his face was grey and dark as a bruised, stormy sky. The hoods of his eyelids hung deep over his eyes. A beard straggled across his cheeks and flies clustered near his lips in a blue-black haze. When he bent down, Horrendo smelled the rum on him, sickly sweet and smothering as a blanket.

'Hand over that treasure, you cut-throat dogs,' hissed the Captain, 'or I'll slice you open like a school of sardines.' The vein in his forehead pounded.

The men watched as he grabbed the sword from the First Mate's side.

They fumbled around in their pockets for the bags of gold, hands shaking with fury and fear. 'Cursin' catfish,' the First Mate couldn't help groaning to Squid, 'but he's hard to kill!'

Horrendo noticed Bombastic squirming next to him, clutching at the pocket of his waistcoat. He looked frantic.

'What have you got there, you thieving mongrel?' The Captain knelt down till his face was inches away from the boy's. 'You wouldn't want to keep anything from your long-lost Captain, would you?'

'No!' protested Bombastic. 'It's nothing, sir. Really!'

As the Captain reached for the small bundle at Bombastic's chest, a bright red blur leapt from the boy's pocket and buried itself in the Captain's beard.

'What the BLAZES—' the Captain opened his mouth to shout.

'No, Pest, no!' cried Bombastic.

But Pest, seeing the open cavern of the Captain's mouth, and swooning with excitement at the smell of rum, hopped straight in.

The men watched with awe as the Captain's face changed from grey to white to crimson. His lids flew up like blinds and his eyes flung open and, although his mouth was stretched wide and the cords of his throat were straining, no sound came out.

'He's chokin' on amphibian!' whispered the First Mate.

'Pest, Pest, come back!' shouted Bombastic. 'Oh, Pet, you'll die in there!'

The Captain flapped at the air, trying to cough, his face turning blue. And then, his chin jutting forward in a spasm, he swallowed.

'My *Pet*!' cried Bombastic. In a frenzy of grief, he reached for the sword the Captain had dropped and started hacking away at the rope that bound him. But the Captain was already swaying with poison, and his hands and feet began to twitch.

'AMPH*IDIOT!*' spluttered the Captain, the jerking movements becoming little jumps, and then he was leaping and running like a madman up the hill.

Bombastic threw off the rope and thundered after him, the sword swiping at the air ahead. 'I'll get you, you lousy devourer of beloved pets,' cried the boy, mad with sorrow. 'You greedy, guzzlin' rum-soaked killer!'

On ran the Captain with lightning speed, shuddering and jerking as he went. Bombastic panted after him, sure that the Captain would drop down in a fit at any moment. What was wrong with the man? Frog poison was supposed to paralyse people, not turn them into marathon runners! But the Captain's feet hardly seemed to touch the ground as he flew along, and soon he was just a dark shape flitting between the bushes.

Indeed, so fast was he going, so full of delirious visions and demon voices was he, the Captain didn't notice the steep rise of the path ahead. He didn't see the sudden spark shooting up from the mountainside above. And he never felt the eerie rumble of the earth underfoot. The only thing the Captain knew was the boiling blood of horror inside him, and the only thing he could do was to run.

It was lucky for Bombastic that he never caught up with the Captain because the next few steps brought the devil man to his end. So crazy with poison and terror and amphibian-loathing was he that he didn't look where he was going and he fell right over the top of the volcano and down, down into the dark smouldering belly below.

When Bombastic finally arrived back at the hut, shoulders stooped with tragedy, face awash with tears, he found only Horrendo waiting anxiously by a pile of neatly coiled ropes.

'I'm so sorry, Bombastic,' Horrendo was saying sympathetically. 'Your dear Pest—only *you* knew all his wonderful qualities, I'm sure. You must feel as if a part of yourself has been lost forever.'

At this, Bombastic crumpled on the ground and howled. Horrendo ventured over and cautiously put an arm around him. 'But remember that Pest died a noble death,' Horrendo went on. 'Pest was a hero. He saved us all from being sliced open like sardines.'

Bombastic nodded. 'It was the rum what did him in, but. Pest was never the same after he went swimmin' in that mug of rum. No sense of danger, y'know? You couldn't talk sense to him any more. The only thing he thought about after that was his rum and where to get more of it. And it was all my fault!'

Bombastic began to cry again and Horrendo rubbed his back. After a while, when the heaving sobs had left him, Bombastic looked up and said, 'Where're the others, then?'

'They've run back down the hill. When the ground shook and the sparks flew, they took fright. They'll be waiting for us down at the shore, you'll see.'

Just then another rumble from the volcano sent the monkeys screeching across the branches above. Horrendo stood up and said, 'We'd better get going too, if you don't mind, that is, because that volcano is definitely active and it's about to blow, I think.'

Bombastic stared at Horrendo. 'You mean you waited for me, when you knew the island could be covered with boilin' lava at any moment? Even though I dobbed you in to the Captain so he made you walk the plank?'

Horrendo looked shyly down at the ground. 'Let's take some of this rope with us, shall we? You never know when a bit of rope will come in handy on a ship, do you?'

And the two boys, swinging a coil over each shoulder, raced down the mountain as the volcano belched mighty firecracker sparks into the night sky.

The moon was rising as the pirates and boys filed back onto the ship. Weary and aching, they tied up the jolly-boat and dinghies again. The First Mate ordered Wicked and Scabrous to hoist the mizzen, as barely a breath of wind ruffled the pewter sea.

Bombastic sniffed a lot as he worked, but everyone pretended they couldn't hear and, once, Rascal patted his hand. Wicked muttered a good deal under his breath but he did what he was told, and fairly nimbly too, so everyone decided they were too tired to deal with him now and the best thing was to ignore him, like a bad smell. Horrendo set about making a nourishing broth and the boys helped clear the deck.

They set sail under a starry sky. Full of soup and dreams of the future, the men lay around the deck, singing, 'My Bonnie Lies Over the Ocean' and 'My Bonny Lass' and 'What I Wouldn't Do for Love'.

'Ain't it strange,' said Bombastic, who was feeling much better now, 'that all these sailor songs are about girls and you never meet any of 'em at sea.'

'That's right,' nodded Wildman, rubbing his chin. 'Do they make women pirates?'

The First Mate nodded. 'They do indeed. We 'ad a fight with a pack of 'em a few years ago. Fierce and nasty lot they were. Their captain took my beard off with her sword.'

The pirates grinned in the dark.

'To tell the truth,' Dogfish said shyly, 'I'm sick of fightin'. I'm tired of me muscles achin' and me indigestion playin' up.'

'I'm the same, an' all,' said Goose. 'I don't want to lose me other pinkie or me head, either.'

'But I could lose it all for love,' sang Buzzard.

'Aye,' agreed Dogfish. 'Can't you just picture it— settling down on dry land, in a nice little house, wakin' up in a woman's arms each mornin'.'

The pirates sighed, imagining.

The boys looked at each other. Rascal whispered something to Horrendo, who cleared his throat.

'You could come back and live in our village,' Horrendo said.

The pirates looked at each other, their eyebrows flying up to their hairlines in amazement.

'You see, once everyone knew that you were living with us,' Horrendo went on as they turned to stare at him, 'you would be like an insurance for our village. Other pirates wouldn't dare come raiding and plundering then, would they? And there's good farming land up in the hills, you know. Why, with your share of the gold, you could all build beautiful houses.'

'Dogfish'd 'ave to do somethin' about his wind problem, but,' teased Squid.

'And how would old Wicked behave in society?' wondered Goose.

'I guess we could keep him chained up in someone's backyard,' suggested Squid, throwing the pirate a lazy punch on the arm.

'By the way, has anyone actually counted all the gold yet?' asked Scabrous, trying to sound merely curious. 'Because I hope with all this *sharing*, there'll still be enough for me to buy me mansion with a sunken bath.'

'I've counted it,' Rip's voice rang out clearly. 'And I'm telling you there's enough gold for everyone to buy ten mansions with twenty sunken baths and gold mirrors besides. So it's best not to go irritatin' everyone, Scabrous, and disturbin' the peace.'

There was silence on the deck as the pirates lay back, thinking of all the splendid things in store for them. Stars glittered like treasure against a black satin sky. Moonlight sparkled on the water. It was good to be alive. The boys stared at Rip in admiration. Rip stared back and didn't even feel like cracking his fingers once.

'You know,' the First Mate said lazily, 'I wouldn't mind me mansion havin' marble mermaids and whatnots lyin' about lookin' curvy and invitin' in the garden.'

'An' I want me own horse in the field like when I was a little nipper,' said Squid.

'And I want me own cook,' said Dogfish.

'And I want servants to fan me when it's hot on account of I got only one earlobe now and it's not as long as Dogfish's,' said Buzzard.

'*What?*' said Goose.

'Aw, stop yer jabberin', we'll 'ave everythin' we want, mateys,' said the First Mate happily. He stretched out his legs and rested his hands behind his head. 'Boy, am I lookin' forward to a home-cooked meal. Can I come an' live right next to you, Horrendo, what do you say?'

But Horrendo was far away, lost in thought. He was imagining their homecoming. His mother and father would run down to the beach, joy lighting their faces, pride sparkling in their eyes. They would be amazed, dazzled, overwhelmed, thrilled. And there right behind them would be Blusta, smiling at him in wonder.

chapter fourteen

And so the great journey ended happily, just as Horrendo had hoped. Of course, there were a few surprises, as life rarely turns out *exactly* as we imagine, does it?

Gretel the Wise Woman came down to the shore with the rest of the villagers the day the ship sailed in. She stood at a distance on the sand, her cat draped around her shoulders, watching mothers and fathers, sisters and brothers drenching the boys with hugs. She smiled a secret smile at parents weeping with joy and boys chattering with excitement and pirates making plans for luxurious lives.

Then she caught Horrendo's eye and beckoned him over.

'You've done well,' she said. 'You have used all that I gave you wisely. And now I will set you free.'

For the second time in his life Horrendo looked deep into her eyes. There he saw pictures from his life in the past and in the future. He saw himself travelling to exotic places; hot countries, snowy mountains. He saw himself as a man, building a house, carrying huge blocks of stone. And there was Rascal's sister, Blusta, planting out a garden just like Gretel's, and mixing her potions.

When the Wise Woman touched his shoulder, her eyes returned to their normal gentle brown, and she smiled at him.

'Thank you,' he said.

'You're welcome,' she said politely, and they both laughed.

Rascal and the other boys drifted over to him then, and with arms linked they strolled up the hill, their astounded parents trailing behind. As they walked, the boys swapped jokes and stories and information about the world as friends do, and very content they were, too, I have to say.

Mind you, it wasn't all 'please' and 'thank you' in the village forever after.

At first, of course, the villagers were relieved and ecstatic that their boys and hard-earned money and kitchen equipment weren't being stolen any more. And naturally, the pirates were overjoyed and boundlessly enthusiastic about the prospect of waking up each morning to a life of comfort and ease.

In fact, so thankful was everyone for their changed lives that they erected a statue of Horrendo in the village square. For the unveiling, his mother baked an enormous cake, big enough for everyone to have a slice. The villagers and pirates all came and shook hands, but it was a bit of a strain being so polite and courteous all the time, and by the end of the night Bombastic's uncle reached a new score of 'thank yous'—256—and broke out in a terrible rash. Hoodlum's dad erupted into boils. A man called Poison, who was the village baker, tried to smile so much that his jaws went into spasm and he couldn't even eat any cake. 'Thievin' devils,' he muttered through clenched teeth every time he had to shake hands with a pirate, 'ought to be hangin' by a noose instead of hangin' out their washin'!'

'Pleased to kill you!' said Mischief's dad as he shook hands with a pirate. He meant to say 'meet you' but his mouth just went the wrong way.

Horrendo began to worry. He'd learnt a lot from his curse of politeness, and knew there were better ways of handling one's rage and fury than pretending it didn't exist. He called everyone into the village square, and had the treasure piled on a table in the centre. The villagers stood close together on one side and the pirates slouched together on the other.

Horrendo's heart trembled as he looked at their scowling faces. Still, he got up on the stool he'd brought and clapped his hands for people's attention. 'Before we share out the gold, everybody, I'd like to tell you about my great idea!'

There was a muttering from all around the square, and Horrendo had to shout to make himself heard. He had just yelled, '*Listen!*' for the fifth time, when Wicked leapt out from the bunch of pirates and grabbed a bag of gold from the pile on the table.

'This'ere is pirate gold,' he cried, waving the bag in the air, 'and no one's goin' to tell me otherwise!'

He looked round wildly for support from the other pirates. 'Finders keepers, losers weepers!' And in great haste he began to pick up two, three, four more bags.

Well, the villagers exploded. Years of hate and misery surged up and overflowed, drowning politeness.

'Oh yeah?' shouted Mischief's dad. 'You're the losers for not listening to Horrendo, you bunch of fish heads. You pirates are so dumb you wouldn't know an idea if it blew a hole through your brain!'

'Shut yer gob, ya soft-bellied layabout!' shouted the pirates, stung.

'Why don't you shut yours, you pack of weevil brains!' bellowed the villagers, outraged.

Voices rang through the square like thunder, crashing over Horrendo, deafening him. Dogfish and Squid came to drag Wicked away, but the damage was done. Villagers and pirates were throwing insults like knives, and soon there'd be blood. There was no hope of plans or peace now, Horrendo knew it.

He stared at Wicked, who was still yelling, held at the wrists by Dogfish. As Horrendo looked he felt a wave of hate building, a boiling anger flushing up to his face and turning it crimson. That greedy, small-minded slug had ruined everything—just like he'd nearly ruined it before. Horrendo saw himself in the hut again, remembered how it had felt to hand the gold over politely, and how Wicked had laughed in his face. All the work of this miraculous journey—they'd survived and returned with gold as well!—and this miserable mangy dog had to go and ruin it all. He could kill him, he could, he could boil his eyes and pickle them...

'You selfish cheating lying pig!' he yelled at Wicked. 'You slimy apology for a human being, you dung beetle, you lousy smear of cockroach pus!' He started to jump up and down on the stool in rage, his blood pounding. 'You greasy ball of frog spawn, you burst boil on the back of the neck, you smelly sock left under the bed to rot, why don't you go stick your head down a snake hole, you greedy gold-guzzling gaby?'

Silence hit the square like a cannonball as Horrendo jumped so hard he broke the stool and fell off. Villagers, pirates and little children stood rigid with surprise, their mouths hanging open. This was Horrendo, their dear sweet Horrendo! *Cursing* now, breaking *furniture*, just like his father before him!

'Oh, my love, are you ill?' Horrendo's mother and father rushed forward to feel his forehead.

'Give the boy some air!' cried Dogfish, handing Wicked over to the First Mate and rushing forward. 'You don't know what he's been through, what with all 'is plank-walkin' and swimmin' under ships an' dodgin' swords. Stand back and let 'im talk. Blessed saint the boy is, and an angel in the galley! Stand back now!'

'Oh yeah, and who are you to give us orders?' Mischief's dad shouted. 'You pirates—you kidnap our children, you rob us and ruin our lives!' He spat on the ground near their feet. 'Who are you to talk of saints?

And now you just expect to sail back in here and order us around!'

'Well, what about you lot?' Dogfish roared back. 'You all sittin' pretty with yer picket fences and yer roses growin' all over 'em and yer hot dinners every night. What've we ever had? We were young lads once too, you know, we was humans with feelings and hearts and everythin' as well.' And Dogfish began to cry.

'Yer just jealous,' muttered Poison the baker, but not so loud.

'Too right we are,' hissed Squid. 'How d'ya think we felt each year sailin' in 'ere and seein' ya with yer children and yer relationships and yer kitchen equipment an' all? And us, slaves to a rum-sodden devil of a Captain who's put callouses on our hands and hearts year after bloody year?'

'Aye, demon that he was,' muttered Buzzard.

'Well, and what do you think *we* felt watching you all striding into our homes and breaking up our families? What was the use of saving our money or rearing our children proper when every time we looked around it was all taken from us?'

There was quiet for a moment as everyone's chests heaved up and down with fury and resentment. Pirates and villagers glared at each other, and the only sound was Dogfish and his sobs turning into hiccoughs.

After a minute the hiccoughs bloomed into great choking sounds and the purple-faced pirate clutched his chest in agony. 'Me indigestion,' he moaned, 'it'll be the death of me.'

'Someone get the man a cup of water,' called out Poison. 'Looks like he's croakin' it right here in front of us.'

Rip ran to the fountain and fetched the water.

Everyone watched Dogfish drink and when he'd finished he wiped his mouth and said, 'Thank you, that saved me life.'

Horrendo looked around at the slightly softened faces and said into the quiet, 'Will you listen to my idea now?'

People nodded and shuffled their feet.

'It's true that we have good reason for hating each other. The pirates have stolen from our village for years, and left us poor and desperate. But it was the Captain who drove them on and he's gone now. His evil soul is buried in the ashes of the volcano.'

The pirates stared at their feet.

'And the men did rescue us boys and bring us back home,' Horrendo went on more quietly now, 'and they've brought treasure to the village as well.'

There was a swell of talk from the villagers, but Horrendo put up his hand. 'So what I propose is that the pirates use their share of the treasure to set up a tavern—the best in the land.'

'Horrendo can be the cooking instructor,' put in Rascal, 'and people will come from all over the country when news of the magnificent food gets about.'

'Yes!' Horrendo went on. 'And then we'll have the money to build proper schools for girls and boys together—imagine, we'd get to have real books and coloured pencils and educational conversations. Why, we'd have games and *fun* like other children have. We'll be the happiest port on the seaboard.'

'Can we still have our Petrifying Pets class, but?' whispered Bombastic to Rascal.

'Yeah,' Rascal whispered back. 'I'm gunna get a hamster.'

The villagers were quiet, thinking. Blusta, who had been staring at Horrendo in admiration, pushed her way through the crowd. She took his hand and held it high.

'This will be the best thing that's ever happened to our miserable little village,' she said, 'and I for one am going to help.' She turned to Horrendo and kissed him loudly on the ear. 'I'll provide your tavern with special herbs from my garden and I think we can rely on Gretel to supply an extra touch of magic.'

Horrendo kissed Blusta right back (not on the ear) and didn't let go of her hand, even when his own grew all warm and sweaty.

'But we'll get to live 'ere in town, right?' said the First Mate loudly. 'In our mansions with the sunken baths?'

And after much discussion amongst the villagers, and some expert Anger Management classes held by Horrendo, that is exactly what they did. The pirates worked happily and no one took a day off for six months except for when Dogfish got engaged to Pandemonium, Bombastic's older sister, and there was a party in the village square.

Lastly, I suppose you're dying to know if Wicked ever learned to behave himself or attended Horrendo's excellent classes in Anger Management?

No, he didn't. He took his share of the treasure and disappeared. The pirates heard news of him occasionally—a bit of diamond-smuggling here, a small war there—and then nothing more.

'Some people never change,' said Rascal, and Horrendo had to agree.